DANGER AT LAKESIDE FARM

DANGER AT LAKESIDE FARM

PATRICIA H. RUSHFORD

MOODY PUBLISHERS

CHICAGO

© 2007 by
PATRICIA H. RUSHFORD

Cover Design: Studio Gearbox.com
Cover Photography: Steve Gardner / PixelWorks Studio
Interior Design: DesignWorks Group (thedesignworksgroup.com)
Editor: Cheryl Dunlop

Library of Congress Cataloging-in-Publication Data

Rushford, Patricia H.
    Danger at Lakeside Farm / by Patricia H. Rushford.
        p. cm. — (Max & me mysteries : bk. 2)
    Summary: When Max becomes the foster child of an elderly woman who grows and makes foods and crafts from lavender, Jessie, still recovering from her bone marrow transplant, not only helps with the business, she also investigates who is trying to shut it down.
    ISBN-13: 978-0-8024-6254-1
    ISBN-10: 0-8024-6254-5
    [1. Friendship—Fiction. 2. Foster home care—Fiction. 3. Business enterprises—Fiction. 4. Leukemia—Fiction. 5. Family life—Washington (State)—Fiction. 6. Washington (State)—Fiction. 7. Mystery and detective stories.] I. Title.

PZ7.R8962Dan 2007
[Fic]—dc22

                                                            2006035512

We hope you enjoy this book from Moody Publishers. Our goal is to provide high-quality, thought-provoking books and products that connect truth to your real needs and challenges. For more information on other books and products written and produced from a biblical perspective, go to www.moodypublishers.com or write to:

Moody Publishers
820 N. LaSalle Boulevard
Chicago, IL 60610

1 3 5 7 9 10 8 6 4 2

Printed in the United States of America

To Andrea Rushford—
my favorite youngest grandchild

AUTHOR NOTE

It may seem strange to some that I would choose heroes like Jessie Miller and Max Hunter—one with leukemia and the other living with an abusive aunt and uncle. I suppose it's because I have cared for children who have suffered and even died with life-threatening illnesses and have worked with children tormented with emotional and physical pain at the hands of abusive adults.

These children were so often brave and resilient and able to overcome great adversity. They showed me what being a hero is all about. As a pediatric nurse and then a counselor, I have always had a heart for children and a desire to help them in any way I can. My earlier nonfiction books *Have you Hugged Your Teenager Today?* and *What Kids Need Most in a Mom,* were written to help and encourage parents in their endeavor to better care for their children. *It Shouldn't Hurt to be a Kid* helps parents, teachers, and caregivers to recognize abuse and to help bring healing to broken children.

Several years ago, I began writing *The Jennie McGrady Mysteries* for kids because I love a good mystery and according to the fan mail I receive, so do kids. My goal has been to provide great, exciting, and adventurous stories, but also to empower kids to rise above the problems they may encounter in life. Jessie and Max do this very well. I hope my readers and fans will enjoy their adventures as much as I have enjoyed writing them.

With Love, Patricia Rushford

www.patriciarushford.com

CHAPTER ONE

J"Jessie, come inside please. Your dad and I need to talk to you." Mom pressed her lips together and ducked back into the house.

Uh-oh. My stomach did a backflip. I couldn't imagine what they wanted to talk about, but right away I thought of my friend, Max Hunter, and wondered what she'd done this time. I scooted away from the table on the porch where I'd been helping my little brother, Sam, put a puzzle together. "I'll be back in a minute," I told him.

"Are you in trouble?" he asked, hope registering in his blue eyes.

"You wish." I hurried inside and pulled out a chair at the kitchen table where my parents were waiting. Dad was playing with the handle of his coffee cup, and Mom had her hands clasped in front of her. "What's wrong? If it's about my room . . ."

"It's not about you, Jessie." Dad glanced up at Mom. Not a good sign. His worried gaze shifted back to me. "It's Max."

I knew it. I looked from one to the other, swallowing back my worst fears.

"Max is missing." Mom took hold of my hand. "Mrs. Truesdale called a few minutes ago. The authorities think she may have run away."

This was way worse than anything I had imagined. "Max wouldn't do that." I could barely talk around the lump in my throat.

"Honey." Dad frowned and took a deep breath. "She is missing, and so is a rather large sum of money. It doesn't look good. They've put out an Amber alert, but . . ."

I jumped up and clenched my fists at my side. "She is not a thief. You should know that." I turned and ran to my room, where I threw some pillows at the floor and then collapsed on the bed. Mom came in to see if I needed anything, then ended up holding me while I sputtered on about Max being innocent.

"I'm sure you're right, Jessie. The police are looking at all the possibilities."

At least she agreed with me, but that didn't make me less miserable. "We have to do something. We can't just sit here."

She hugged me tighter. "I know it's hard, but there's really nothing we can do, except pray and let the police do their jobs."

I didn't want to accept that, but I didn't have much choice. I washed my face and went back out to the porch, where I tried to focus on the puzzle.

Later, during the five o'clock news, I sat in front of the television set trying to figure out where my best friend might be and praying that God would keep her safe.

According to the news anchor, "local officials" were saying that Max Hunter had been a troubled girl. They also said she was wanted for questioning in a recent theft and vandalism act. *Had been?* They made it sound like she was dead.

The accusations infuriated me. I knew Max hadn't stolen or vandalized anything, and I doubted Max had run away. But how could I prove it? Part of what they were saying was too true. Max did have a troubled past. She'd been abused and had lived with an aunt and uncle who did drugs. I had to admit that running away was something she might do, but not without telling me. Well, she might do that too, I realized. But she would never steal. Never.

As much as I wanted to believe my declarations of innocence on Max's part, doubt seeped into my mind like water into a leaky boat. More than anything, I wanted to believe in Max, but with all that had happened in the last few days, I couldn't be sure.

Max had changed a lot since she first moved to Chenoa Lake. She'd been wild and crazy at first, wearing outrageous mismatched clothes and coloring her hair every shade known to humankind—sometimes all at once. I eventually learned that the clothes mostly came from thrift shops. Still, Max made up her own rules about what to wear. No one in our sixth-grade class at Lakeview School likes Max much, but I think that's because she doesn't especially want them to. Max has a prickly side and isn't afraid to show it.

For some reason Max and I hit it off—maybe because I don't fit in any more than she does. See, I have leukemia. That in itself isn't a huge thing, but during my chemo treatments, my hair fell out and never grew back. Anyway, most kids in school ignore me, like they're afraid they'll catch the cancer too. Some of the girls are mean. Part of the problem is mine, I guess. Max tells me I can be a little prickly too. I like to think I'm just being honest.

And speaking of honesty, I wished now Max hadn't gone to live with Amelia Truesdale. Maybe if I'd thrown a fit the day she told me about her plans, she would have stayed with us and not gotten herself into this mess.

But wait—I'm getting ahead of myself. This fiasco with Max and Mrs. Truesdale started about a week ago—the day before I got out of the hospital after having a bone marrow transplant.

CHAPTER TWO

Max had come to the hospital to see me like she did most days. She hitched herself up on the edge of my bed and blew a bubble with her fat glob of raspberry bubble gum. "When are you getting out of here?"

"Maybe tomorrow," I said. "I hope so anyway."

"Good." The bubble popped and covered most of her freckled nose. She peeled it off, shoved it back into her mouth, and kept chewing. Max heaved a deep sigh like she was bored, then got up and walked to the window.

Max is about a foot taller than me and almost as thin. She's actually normal in height—I'm short, or petite as my mother likes to say. She had on loose cargo pants with a ton of pockets—her favorite style—and a baggy blue tie-dyed T-shirt. My mother says she bought Max some new clothes, but I haven't seen them yet. She looks like a boy from the back with her hair all stubbly. It's actually kind of cute, but the style had not been hers by choice. Her aunt had shaved all of her hair off to punish her for something. It's growing back in, and so far Max hasn't tried to color it.

I think her hair is brown with red highlights, but I'm not sure yet.

"Why do you want to know when I'm going home?" I asked.

Max turned back to me—a distant look in her eyes. "Huh? Oh, nothing. I just wondered."

It must have been frustrating to have me take so long to get well. Unfortunately, having a bone marrow transplant is not a quick fix. I'd been in the hospital for more than a month, and so far, everything seemed to be going okay, but I still needed to be careful. The doctors say my immune system is still *fragile.* All that to say, I have about as much strength as a stalk of overcooked asparagus.

I wondered if Max had found another girlfriend to hang around with. I hoped not. Right away I pulled the thought back in. I wasn't being fair. *Just because I'm stuck here doesn't mean Max can't make new friends.*

The way Max was acting, I could tell she was up to something. But then, my friend was always up to something. Since Max and I had become friends this spring, I'd gotten into more trouble than at any other time in my life. Of course, some of that trouble had been my own fault. But that's another story.

"I've been thinking." Max came back and settled herself in the chair beside my bed. She didn't like sitting still and seemed even more restless than usual.

"That could be dangerous." I smiled at her.

She shot me a look that said she didn't appreciate my attempt at humor. "If you're going to be such a smart mouth, I won't tell you." She blew another bubble and reined it in.

"I'm sorry," I said.

"No, you're not." Max grinned, showing the small gap between her two front teeth.

"So tell me what you've been thinking about." I leaned back into my pillow, trying not to look as tired as I felt.

"You're not going to like it."

"Tell me."

She blew another bubble. "Okay. I'm thinking about moving into the foster home Child Services found for me."

"You are?" I didn't bother to hide my shock or my disappointment. I didn't want Max to leave, and I thought going into a foster home was the last thing she'd do. That's what she'd told me. "I thought you were going to stay with us." To be honest, I didn't even know she'd been thinking about moving out. She'd been living at my house while I'd been in the hospital trying to get strong enough to go home. I'd even talked to my parents about letting her stay with us permanently. Guess that wasn't going to happen. I wondered if my parents had pressured her.

"Don't take it personally, Jess," Max said.

"Who is it?" I asked, probably sounding as annoyed as I felt. I didn't much like being left out of a decision as important as that.

"Mrs. Truesdale."

"You're kidding." Her announcement surprised me, and for more reasons than one. I knew Amelia Truesdale and couldn't see where she and Max had anything in common. Amelia, as she insisted everyone call her, was as much of an antique as our church.

She'd been going to Saint Luke's since it was built in 1923, or almost that long. "Mrs. Truesdale doesn't seem like the parental type," I said. "She has to be at least 90."

"So?" Max pushed herself out of the chair again and paced over to the window and back. "She's 79."

I shrugged. I suppose age shouldn't really matter. Mrs. Truesdale has outlived three husbands, and she's still living on her 50-acre lavender farm and gardens. "How did . . . ? I mean, why would . . . ?"

"Why would she want me?" Max lowered her gaze to the floor. "I don't know. Maybe it's because the state pays people for taking in rejects."

"That's not what I was going to say." It made me mad when Max got down on herself like that. "And you are not a reject." I may as well have been talking to a fence post. She'd gone over to the window again and was staring at something outside. It seemed to me that Mrs. Truesdale was too old to be a foster mom, and I told Max that.

"My caseworker said something about Amelia being a special case. Or maybe I'm the special case. I'm not sure, but I guess she's certified."

I understood how she'd come to see herself as a reject. Max was an orphan and probably had good reason to feel that way. Her parents had died in a plane crash, and then she'd had the bad luck of living with an aunt and uncle who were lousy parents. To make matters even worse, she'd been placed in a foster home once and had been abused there too. I'd helped her get away from her aunt and uncle, and I think she appreciated that. She misses them, but like she told me, she's happy they're getting the help they need.

"Do you like Mrs. Truesdale?" I asked.

Max shrugged and turned around to face me. "I only met her once. She seems nice enough, but I need to talk to her. Get to know her. I want you to go out there with me."

"Sure." I took a drink from the glass of water on the bedside stand and then scooted back up in the bed. Max wanted my opinion, and I appreciated that, but I still didn't like the idea.

"Like you said, she's pretty old." Max folded her arms.

"I thought you said age didn't make any difference to you."

She frowned and sat back down in the chair. "It doesn't, but what if she croaks while I'm there? What if my hanging around is too much for her?"

"Oh, Max, I doubt that."

Max chewed on her lower lip. "I'm not thinking about living with her because I need a parent. I'd be doing it to help her out with chores and stuff."

I had to smile. Max had a good heart, and I was beginning to see benefits for both Max and Amelia.

"She's too old to be living out there alone," Max went on.

"She isn't exactly alone," I reminded her. "She has a hired hand—Carlos Sanchez."

"Carlos isn't there anymore. He left about three weeks ago and didn't tell anyone where he was going. No one has seen him since."

"Carlos is gone?" Carlos had been a member at Saint Luke's. That's how he and Mrs. Truesdale had connected. He'd been a migrant worker and was glad for the permanent job. He helped her to harvest the lavender and take care of the farm.

"It happened while you were still at the hospital in Seattle," Max said.

"Are the police trying to find him?"

"I guess. Turns out he's an illegal immigrant and they think maybe he moved out of the area to keep from getting deported."

"No kidding." I'd known Carlos for two years and couldn't imagine him just leaving. While I was trying to digest this strange piece of news, Max said, "Mrs. T hired another guy. Martin something."

Maybe it was just my imagination, but I had a feeling something wasn't right. I just didn't know at the time how *not right* it would be.

CHAPTER THREE

Max didn't seem to notice my concern over Carlos and kept talking.

"Heidi Ellis says Mrs. T and I would be good for each other." Max sounded as though she were still trying to talk herself into moving.

"Who is Heidi?" I asked.

"Oh, I forgot. You haven't met her. She's my social worker . . . um, the lady from Child Protective Services."

"I thought you didn't like her."

"Yeah, well, she was just doing her job, and she did let me stay at your place. She's kind of like your mom and dad in a way. Heidi talks to me like my opinions matter." Max swung her skinny legs back and forth and pressed her hands on the edge of the seat. She seemed nervous, and I didn't blame her. Going into a foster home was a big step for her, especially considering what she'd been through before.

"I don't understand," I said. "You like my parents, and they like you. Why do you even want to move? Did my parents say something to make you think they didn't want you?"

"No. I just think it's the right thing to do."

"Hmm." I tried to picture Max living with Mrs. Truesdale. Her farm was only a few miles out of town on Salmonberry Road. Like so many places in our area, including my house, part of it bordered on Chenoa Lake. I'd never been inside Amelia's house, but I had always wanted to. It's a two-story Victorian, painted light yellow with white trim. It looks like a dollhouse with all of the gingerbread trim. She has a little roadside stand that's open to the public in the summertime. My mom and I have stopped there a few times. "When would you move out there?" I asked.

"As soon as I tell Heidi what I want to do."

"I still don't know why you'd even want to leave. Are my parents too—you know . . . ?"

"Parental?" Max offered.

"Yeah, like too strict? I know with your aunt and uncle you could do pretty much what you wanted."

She shrugged. "Your mom and dad are nice, but they have a lot of restrictions. I don't want to do anything wrong, but I'm feeling kind of smothered. I think they're worried I'll be a bad influence on Sam." She chuckled. "Personally, I think Sam is a bad influence on me."

I had to agree. My five-year-old brother was cute, but mischievous. "I don't think they need to worry."

"No kidding. He's even teaching me a few things."

"Like what?"

"Oh, nothing." She raised her eyebrows and I knew she and

Sam had something planned for my homecoming.

"I can't wait to get home," I said. For part of my hospital stay, I'd been too sick to care. Now I was looking forward to Mom's cooking and my own bed, and even my pesky little brother. I was even looking forward to seeing my next-door neighbor, Ivy, who had snubbed me for most of this past school year. Then all of a sudden just before school let out for the summer, she started being nice. She invited me to a party, but I couldn't go, so she decided to postpone it until I was well enough to come.

And I wanted to see Cooper Smally, the guy who bullied everyone he met and had even fewer friends than Max and me. He'd turned from being my worst enemy to being a friend. I wondered if he'd be hanging out with Max and me much this summer. I think he likes Max—but I don't think Max feels the same way.

"Is Cooper home from that camp he went to?" He and his dad had gone to a camp in Oregon right when school got out, so he hadn't come to see me since I got the transplant. He'd sent me a get-well card, though, which I still had sitting on the shelf above the sink with the others.

"Nope. I haven't seen him." Max got up and came to stand beside my bed. "I need to go."

"Sure." I didn't want her to leave, but she'd been there almost an hour.

"I'm glad you're feeling better."

"Me too." I watched her leave, then leaned back into my pillow and closed my eyes. I hated to admit it, but visitors still tired me out. I sighed and hoped I wouldn't always be this way.

The next morning my doctor gave me the all clear and told my parents they could take me home. My prognosis—that's their medical term for predicting my future—was good, whatever that meant. Some kids do great after bone marrow transplants. Some don't. I've decided I'm going to get completely well and live as long as Mrs. Truesdale. I think it would be cool to be a normal kid again. At least that's what I'm praying for.

CHAPTER FOUR

"We ordered sunshine for you, Princess." Dad winked at me in the rearview mirror on our drive home.

I smiled. "Thanks."

On our drive through town, I was amazed at how different everything looked from just a few weeks ago. Spring had turned to summer, and I loved summers at the lake. Downtown the stores looked even better than last year. Flowers of all colors filled the planter boxes and overflowed their mossy hanging baskets. Music poured from the speakers by the amphitheater that overlooked the lake.

The wooden signs at each end of town proclaimed that our town was *A Little Piece of Heaven.* I suppose that was true in a way. Chenoa Lake, along with two other small towns, Lakeside and Hidden Springs, lies at the base of the Cascade Mountains on one of the most beautiful lakes in Washington state. The lake covers some ten thousand acres, and we live at the northeast end. Most of the land surrounding the lake is national forest and is as wild as the dozens of species of animals and birds that live there.

Dad stopped at one of main street's three traffic lights. We watched a tall, clean-shaven man in a dark suit and tie walk out of the real estate office and cross the street. He looked out of place all dressed up. I watched him angle over to one of those expensive black Cadillac Escalades. He looked like a hit man for the mob. I almost suggested that Dad stop and check up on the realtor, Charlie O'Donnell. But, since my dad waved at the man, I thought I'd better keep my imaginative musings to myself. "Who's that, Dad?" I asked instead.

"John Porter. A potential customer."

"He looks rich. Are you designing a house for him?" My dad is an architect.

Dad laughed and stepped on the gas when the light turned green. "He is rich. The house—or mansion—he wants will run around three-quarters of a million."

I hoped my dad got the job. With all my medical bills, we owe a lot of money.

"Why didn't Max and Sam come with you to pick me up?" I asked my parents.

Mom turned around and smiled at me. "They're planning something for your homecoming, but I'm sworn to secrecy." She brushed her thick dark hair behind her ear. My mother, Amy Miller, is a professional artist and looks like it. Most of the time, she wears flowing dresses with Birkenstocks, and she almost always has a paint smudge somewhere on her face or arms.

"Did Max tell you she might be moving in with Mrs. Truesdale?" I asked.

"She did." My father answered this time. "I'm not sure it's a good idea. Max needs more supervision than what Amelia can give her."

"I disagree," Mom said. "Max has been pretty much on her own for a long time. I think being with Amelia will tame her and make her more responsible. And Amelia could use the company and the extra help. Except for the workers she hires, she's been alone since her kids moved out. And that son of hers . . ."

Her angry tone when she mentioned Amelia's son got my attention. I didn't know she had a son. "What do you mean?" I asked.

Dad gave Mom a this-isn't-a-discussion-to-be-having-in-front-of-the-kids look. Mom said, "If Max is moving in with her, Jessie will find out sooner or later."

"What?" I leaned forward as much as my seat belt would allow.

"That poor woman." Mom sighed. "She has two children. The daughter lives back east somewhere—Minnesota, I think. She comes to visit about once a year, if that. Amelia's son lives in Portland and has two children and I think three grandchildren." Mom hesitated. "It's really a very sad story . . ."

"And you'll have to save it for later." Dad pulled into the drive-way. "Will you look at that?"

CHAPTER FIVE

"Oh, wow!" I squealed. There in the front yard was a huge banner that read *Welcome Home Jessie.* It was decorated with wild splashes of red, yellow, and green and strung up between two trees. Max, Sam, and Ivy were blowing party horns and carrying balloons and cheering like I'd just made a home run or something. I have to say it was the best welcome home I've ever had.

The kids took the balloons and noisemakers into the back-yard. Dad carried me through the house and out to the back deck before putting me down. The table was all decorated, and some-one had made a cake. At least that's what I imagined it had been. Unfortunately, we wouldn't be eating any of it. Ivy's boxer, Deeogee, had pulled the tablecloth off the table and was in the process of licking the last few chocolate crumbs off the plate. The dog's odd name was actually just the spelling of d-o-g.

"Oh, no!" Ivy screamed as she ran toward the dog.

Deeogee looked at her with huge brown eyes, whimpered, and ducked. Pieces of frosting and cake crumbs fell from his mouth and nose. Talk about getting caught with the goods.

"He does this all the time." Ivy grabbed his leash and turned back to us. There were tears in her eyes. "I'm so sorry. I had him tied up, but he must have worked himself loose."

"It's okay, Ivy." I started laughing. "He looks so guilty and . . ." Then we were all laughing. I laughed so hard my knees buckled and I dropped onto them. I had tears in my eyes, too, and my stomach hurt, but the laughing didn't stop. Finally after rolling around on the ground for a few minutes, the laughter faded. I held my aching stomach and groaned. I hadn't had a good laugh in a long, long time.

"Jessie, are you all right?" Dad kneeled down beside me, placed his arms under my neck and knees, and lifted me up.

"I'm fine. This is so cool, even if Deeogee did eat the cake."

He grinned. "I'm glad you find it amusing."

"The cake wasn't that great-looking anyway," Max said, eyeing the dog with disdain. "I can make another one."

Mom brushed her hair back. "That's all right." She settled an arm around Max's shoulders. "It's the thought that counts. We'll have plenty to eat with our picnic lunch. And I have ice cream and fresh strawberries for dessert."

"Ivy," Dad said, "I think you'd better have your parents call the vet. I'm not sure what eating an entire cake will do to his system."

Ivy sighed and pulled on Deeogee's leash. "I'll take him home, where I should have left him in the first place. Dad will know what to do. We have to keep everything out of his reach or he eats it. Last Halloween he got into the candy and ate it all, even the wrappers." She frowned and shook her index finger at him. "You are a naughty dog."

Deeogee licked her hand as if to apologize, but I had a hunch it was really to slurp up the frosting on Ivy's fingers.

I started laughing again.

"Don't encourage him." Ivy rolled her eyes and headed for their yard next door.

While Ivy was gone, Mom and Max cleaned up the mess Deeogee had made and then reset the table. They put out plates, and some veggies and chips for us to nibble on. Dad heated up the grill and put on the chicken. My mouth watered when I thought about how good everything would taste. Hospital food is about as tasteless as wallpaper paste. Not that I've ever eaten wallpaper paste.

While everybody was busy getting the food ready, including Sam, who had the job of setting the table, I went inside and got my special quilt and pillow from the basket near the patio door, then curled up on the porch swing to watch. The trip home and all the laughing had worn me out, but in a nice way.

Being home again and watching my family made my heart glad. I loved moments like this because they made me want to live for a long time.

I closed my eyes for a second and the next thing I knew, Mom was on the swing beside me, kissing my forehead and brushing back my nonexistent hair. "Time to eat, sweetie." She smiled down at me and squeezed my hand. "Are you up to joining us at the table, or do you want me to bring you a tray?"

"I'll eat with you." Looking across the lawn, I saw that everyone was already seated and waiting for me. Everyone included Ivy, Max, and my family. I wished Cooper could have been there. I didn't know when he and his dad were coming home.

I felt a little shaky when I stood up, so Mom put her arm around my waist and walked with me, then held on to me until I sat down.

"Okay, Sam," Dad said. "I think we're ready."

Sam punched the air and sang, "Thank You God for giving us food . . ." to the tune of the original *Superman* theme song. Everyone laughed at his antics. He went a little crazy and climbed up on the table to show us he could fly. Dad grabbed him around the waist and sat him back down. "C'mon, Buddy. You can fly later. Right now it's time to eat."

Sam put his elbows on the table and cupped his chin in his hands. Heaving a heavy sigh, he said, "Okay."

"Will you be able to come to my party on Friday?" Ivy asked as we started clearing the table after we'd eaten.

"Sure. I think so." I glanced over at my mother.

"As long as you don't overdo," she said. "Since you'll be right next door it should be okay. But, Jessie, you need to promise to come home if you start feeling too tired."

I rolled my eyes at the all-too-familiar warning. "I know." She'd invited Max, too, and I was a little nervous about what might happen. I don't know if I was worried about the other girls doing something to Max and me, or if I was worried about Max doing something to them.

Ivy turned to Max. "Have you decided yet?"

Max shrugged. "I'll probably come. I'll need to make sure it's okay with Mrs. Truesdale."

"Does that mean you've made up your mind?" I thought Max wanted me to go with her to talk to Amelia.

"Why would you ask Amelia?" Ivy picked up another plate to add to the stack.

Max told her about possibly moving in with the older woman. To me she said, "I'll decide for sure after I go to her house with you."

"Neat." Ivy seemed glad that Max might be leaving, and that annoyed me. I hadn't said anything more, and I probably wouldn't, but I was still upset that Max would rather live with Amelia Truesdale than with us.

Max took a load of plates into the house, and Ivy and I started carrying in glasses and silverware. "Amelia is a nice lady," Ivy said, "but she's had some problems lately."

"Like what?" I asked. Ivy knew Amelia Truesdale better than I did because Ivy's mother owned the Alpine Tea and Candy Shoppe where Amelia sold a lot of her lavender products.

"The guy who worked for her left, and she had to do a lot of the work herself until she could find someone else. That meant she couldn't spend as much time baking stuff for the shop, and that means less money. Less money means she can't pay her bills."

"I heard about Carlos, but she has a new guy, right?"

Ivy nodded. "Last time she was in, I overheard her telling Mom that her son wants her to sell the farm and go into a home."

"Like a nursing home?" I asked.

"Something like that." Ivy frowned. "Maybe it was a retirement home. Anyway, Mom was pretty upset. She told Amelia there's no way he could make her move against her will."

Could he? I wondered. I thought about what Ivy had said and decided to ask my mom and dad about it later. I needed to tell Max too. If there was a chance that Amelia would end up in a nursing home, she shouldn't be taking Max in. One thing was for sure—I didn't want to see Max hurt again, and I'd do whatever it took to make sure that didn't happen.

CHAPTER SIX

We finished cleaning up, and Max suggested we take the rowboat out on the lake. Ivy said she needed to go home and clean her room and then go to work at the shop. Sam was already playing with the twins next door, so that left Max and me.

"You're going to have to row all the way," I reminded Max as I slipped a life jacket over my head and put on a navy blue and white scarf. Mom always made me wear something on my head when it was sunny.

"Don't worry," Max said. "After what happened to you last time, I may never let you row the boat again."

Dad yelled a warning not to go too far. Not that he had to. I'd learned the hard way that the lake sometimes has a mind of its own when it comes to currents and wind conditions.

I trailed my hands in the water, feeling a little nervous as Max rowed away from the dock. Seeing as how I'd been stranded out there on an island for nearly two whole days, I would probably be afraid of the lake for some time.

Max headed up the lake, looking as though she had a mission. "Going somewhere special?" I asked.

"Yeah." Max screwed her face up a little as she rowed, like she was concentrating really hard on something. "I thought we'd row by Mrs. T's place."

"Is something going on that you haven't told me about?"

Max stopped rowing for a second. "Yeah, but I'm not sure I should tell you."

"What?" I hated when people said something like that and wouldn't talk. "You have to tell me now."

"All right." She started rowing again. "There's something going on with her. I'm not sure what it is. Heidi seemed worried but wouldn't tell me. No one likes to say anything to kids. Did you know Mrs. Truesdale brings her lavender tea and scones and gifts and stuff in to the tea shop for Mrs. Cavanaugh to sell?"

I said that I did. "I bought some of her soap and potpourri for my mom once." Amelia makes lavender-scented sachets with all kinds of neat material. She also makes lavender tea, jams, syrups, and scones that she sells at her roadside stand and at the tea shop.

Remembering my conversation with Ivy, I told Max what Ivy had said about the money and about Amelia's son. My finger snagged on a water lily tendril that had stretched itself from a clump growing close to shore. I pulled my hand in.

"That fits," Max said. "I was looking at all the stuff Mrs. T made and overheard Mrs. Cavanaugh talking to a lady who came in asking for Amelia's Lavender Scone Mix. Mrs. C didn't have any, and the lady seemed disappointed. Then she told her that Amelia was worried about losing the farm. She hasn't been able to make her mortgage payments for two months."

"That's terrible. Did she say why?"

Max chewed her lip. "She said something about Amelia's son wanting her to move into that place for old people in town. I couldn't quite hear everything because she lowered her voice. I wonder why he wants to force her to move."

"Ivy said he wanted Amelia to sell the property," I said. "You know how expensive those new places on the lake are. If her son talked her into selling the place to a developer or developed it himself, he could make millions."

"You could be right. Maybe he wants to get his mother out of the way so he can sell the land. Only what if she refuses to move or to sell? What can he do about that?"

I didn't know. "Mom might know something. When we were driving home from the hospital, she mentioned the son. She was going to tell me the story, but we were just pulling into the driveway. We'll have to remember to ask when we get back."

We eased up to Mrs. Truesdale's dock. Max got out and had started tying up the boat when we heard someone scream.

CHAPTER SEVEN

Max took off running. I managed to get out of the boat and hurried after her. Mrs. Truesdale was lying facedown in a large pile of lavender. An Australian shepherd circled Max, barking furiously. The older woman rolled over and started laughing.

"What happened?" Max asked. "We were on the lake and heard you scream."

"That was Nubie's doing." She pointed to a multicolored goat with its mouth full of flowers. "I was bending over to pick up some lavender and that fool goat butted me right where I sit down." She reached up and took Max's extended hand. "Thank you, dear." To the dog, she said, "Hush, Molly. I'm okay, and these girls are friends."

Friends. I liked that, and I liked the way her blue eyes crinkled at the corners.

The dog pushed at Max's hand, apparently wanting to be petted and reassured. Max knelt down and let Molly lick at her face. When Molly came over to me, I slid my hand over her silky fur, wishing I could let her lick my face too, but I couldn't. Just petting animals could be dangerous. I'd need to wash my hands soon. That was one of the things the nurses and my mother had drilled into my head. I had to be careful about what I touched and always be aware of the germs I came in contact with.

Mrs. Truesdale brushed the flowers from her clothes and picked several blossoms out of her hair. This was a side of Amelia Truesdale I'd never seen. She was wearing jeans and a plaid short-sleeved blouse. From the dirt stains on her face and arms, and the damp silver-gray curls pressed around her sweaty face, I imagined she'd been working for several hours. She chuckled again. "What a picture we must have made."

"Are you sure you're okay, Mrs. T?" Max asked, apparently not seeing the humor.

"I'm fine. I imagine I'll have a few bruises tomorrow, but at the moment nothing is injured except my pride. And please, call me Amelia."

I don't think Max believed her. "Maybe you should go see a doctor."

She straightened and looked Max in the eye. "I appreciate your concern, dear, but there's nothing to worry about." She picked up the large straw hat she'd apparently been wearing and slapped it against her leg. "Would you girls like some cookies and milk or tea? I could use a break, and I would love the company."

"Sure," I said, even though I was still pretty full from lunch.

When we went inside, Molly stopped at the doorway and curled up on the rug. I excused myself to go to the bathroom and wash my hands. Max and Mrs. Truesdale washed up, too, before going back into the kitchen.

"What brings you girls up this way?" Amelia asked as she set a plateful of cookies on the table. We'd both opted for peach lemonade rather than milk, so she brought us each a full glass and poured one for herself.

"Curiosity," Max blurted out. "We wanted to see your place from the lake side."

"Sizing it up, eh?" Amelia smiled.

"Yeah." Max took a cookie and bit into it. "Hmm. This is awesome."

"I'm glad you like it. It's my new recipe for lavender shortbread cookies. I'll be mixing up the dry ingredients and packaging it. I must say, though, adding another product seems a bit daunting at the moment."

"You could sell millions of these." I took a sip of my drink to wash the bite of cookie down. The lemonade was good too, and I said so.

"Thank you. It's three bags of peach tea with lemon, sugar, and water."

She sat down with us and sipped at her drink. "Before you go, remind me to package up some cookies for you to take home. I'd like your family's opinion, Jessie."

"They'll love them."

"Would you girls like a tour of the house when we've finished our snack?"

"I would." I probably sounded a little too eager.

"That would be cool." Max didn't sound all that excited. She had that worried look on her face again.

Amelia must have noticed. "Is everything all right, Max?"

"I guess. I was just wondering how much money you'd get from the state if I came to live with you."

Amelia sat up straighter and seemed surprised. I didn't blame her. Sometimes Max talked before she thought. "Why, I don't know. Isn't that funny? I suppose I should have asked, but to be honest, the subject of money didn't come up. Now that I think about it, I suppose they do offer some money for your expenses."

Max nodded and seemed pleased with her answer.

Amelia tipped her head slightly. "I hope you weren't thinking I wanted you for the money."

"I guess I was," Max admitted. "Some foster parents are just in it for the money and the work they can get out of the kids."

Amelia smiled. "Did you know that I contacted Child Services, Max? I asked specifically about you."

"You did? But how did you even know?"

She laughed. "Mrs. Cavanaugh was telling me about your living with the Millers. I talked to your mother too, Jessie. I've thought before about being a foster parent, but never got around to it. I said to myself, 'Amelia, you are not getting any younger. And it looks as though this young lady could use a home.' So, I called CPS."

Max has a home, I wanted to say, but didn't. I wondered if Ivy's mother had talked about Max because she didn't want Max living next door to them. Did she see Max as a troublemaker? Why else would she mention Max to Mrs. Truesdale? Had my own mother complained?

Max finished off her peach lemonade and snagged another cookie. "I've made up my mind." She looked at me and then at Amelia. "If you still want me to live with you, I will."

Amelia smiled. "I do indeed, Max."

I had a sick feeling in the pit of my stomach. *No, Max,* I wanted to say. *It's too soon.* But I kept my mouth shut. Amelia Truesdale was a very nice lady, and living on a farm would be a great experience for Max. I almost wished I could stay with her and wondered how Amelia would feel about my visiting sometimes. Like every day.

"You're awfully quiet, Jessie," Amelia said. "Am I right in thinking you don't want Max to be so far away?"

"I want Max to be happy," I said. And I did. I was being selfish in wanting her to live at my house.

"Don't worry, dear. You're welcome to come as often as you like."

I pasted a pretend smile on my face. I probably should have felt better, but I didn't. I had a feeling Max would find too many fun things to do here. After a while, she'd forget about me.

When I finished my drink, Amelia gave us a tour of the house. It was as pretty inside as out. My mom gets *Victoria Magazine,* and I thought Amelia's house looked just like some of the pictures I'd seen in it. It looked like springtime, with pastel colors and flowers.

Downstairs, Amelia showed us the living room, then the craft room. There were a lot of dried bunches of lavender hanging from hooks in the ceiling, a sewing machine, cabinets, and a bunch of material. The place smelled like a florist shop. "In case you haven't already figured it out, this is where I do all my crafts."

Max and I wandered around the room as she showed us the lavender sachets, wands, and soaps. From there she led us back into the living room and started up the staircase, her hand on the carved wooden banister.

Some of the boards squeaked when we stepped on them. Amelia said, "This old house has a lot of creaks and groans. You'll get used to them."

She opened double doors into the master bedroom. "Come on in." We followed her inside. The room had a rounded area with a cushioned chair and a chaise longue. There was an end table and a basket full of books and magazines, and another basket of knitting. "This is the turret room," she explained, "and my bedroom."

"Cool." Max turned around in a circle.

"You must read a lot," I said, seeing the wall of built-in bookshelves.

"When I can. You girls are welcome to read any of my books. I have quite a collection."

"Your room sure is big," Max said.

"This used to be a four-bedroom house, but I had it redone a few years ago because the rooms were so small. Now I have two large rooms up here plus two bathrooms. My bathroom is in here. It's the only one with a tub, but you're welcome to use it whenever you want."

"Showers are fine with me," Max said. "Do you ever get tired of purple?"

Amelia laughed. "Never. I've always loved shades of lavender from the palest to the darkest." We followed her out of the room and down the hall to the next door on the opposite side of the house.

"So this would be my room?" Max asked when Amelia opened the door to let us in. The hallway floor creaked three times as we walked inside.

"It would. I hope you like it. I recently had it painted and put in new furnishings."

The room was almost as big as Amelia's, but it was done all in white with bright-colored cushions and accents. I recognized one of the pictures on the wall as one my mother had painted.

"Wow," Max exclaimed. "It even has a bathroom."

"Actually, that bath has two entries. You can get to it from the hall too."

My legs were getting tired, and I sat down on the bright yellow chair in the corner of the room.

"You okay, Jess?" Max asked. Turning to Mrs. Truesdale, she said, "Jessie just got out of the hospital today. I probably should take her back home."

"I'm not tired." I chewed on the inside of my cheek, trying not to sound like a cranky little kid. I didn't appreciate when Max got parental on me. "But we probably should go. If my dad doesn't see our boat on the lake he'll probably call out the search-and-rescue team."

Amelia nodded. "Well, you can't blame him for being concerned considering all you've been through."

"I guess." I smiled even though I didn't feel like it. I wasn't sure if her *considering* meant because I was sick or because of my error in judgment, which was what my father called it, when I took the boat out on the water by myself and got lost.

"When would you like to move in, Max?" Amelia asked.

Max shrugged. "Tomorrow?"

No! I couldn't believe Max was moving so soon. She'd told me she wanted my opinion, but she hadn't even asked me what I thought. *And what about Amelia's son? Shouldn't we find out what's going on first?* I tried to project my thoughts to Max, but she seemed to have forgotten I was in the room. I felt Max slipping away, and there didn't seem to be anything I could do about it.

CHAPTER EIGHT

"Tomorrow would be wonderful," Amelia said. "But can you get packed that quickly?"

Max chuckled. "It's not like I have a ton of stuff."

She hesitated. "Well then. We'll need to check with your case-worker to be sure, but it should be okay. Tomorrow it is. I'll pick you up around ten."

I felt numb and cold and insignificant, and I wished Max had just come alone. Well, not really. I liked Amelia Truesdale, and I liked her house and her tea and her cookies. We went back downstairs where Amelia packaged up some cookies. Max snatched another one from the nearly empty plate. Amelia offered me one, but my stomach hurt too much.

"Be safe, girls." Amelia waved at us from the doorway. "I'll call your parents, Jessie, and let them know you're on your way."

"Thanks, Mrs. T." Max seemed to be in a good mood, which made me feel even worse. I wanted to be happy for her. I really did, but I feared I might be losing her as a friend. Maybe not today, but soon.

Mom was putting away her gardening supplies when we rowed up to the dock. "Hey, you two. You should have told me you were going to Amelia's place. I have a book she loaned me that I need to return."

"We didn't know." Max helped me out of the boat while she told Mom about the goat that had butted Amelia into the big pile of lavender. Even though I was still upset with Max, I had to laugh at the way she told it.

"I'm glad she wasn't hurt." Mom eyed the bag I had in my hand. "Are those the cookies? You didn't eat them all, did you?"

"No, but they sure are good," Max answered for me again. I felt like telling her my body might be tired, but my mouth was still working. I didn't say anything though. Since this was going to be her last night here, I didn't want to get her mad at me. In fact, on the ride back to the house, I'd pretty much decided that my bad mood was on account of my being tired and trying to do too much too soon. Maybe my worries about Max moving in with Amelia were on account of that.

Mom took the cookies and wrapped an arm around my shoulders. "You look exhausted, sweetheart." She opened the package and smelled it.

"I'm fine." I sounded more grouchy than I meant to.

"Why don't you nap while Max and I get dinner ready?" She bit into a cookie. "Hmm, these are heavenly."

"That's what we thought," Max said. "Mrs. T is thinking about packaging the mix and selling them in the tea shop."

"Oh, I think these will go over big. I can see them selling all over the country."

Max laughed. "That would be a lot of cookies."

Mom took another bite. "I wonder if Amelia has thought about expanding her business. I can see a huge market for everything she makes. I'll have to talk to her about it."

We helped Mom carry her supplies up to the house. I set the paint box on the deck and went inside for my quilt and pillow. I closed my eyes while Max told Mom she'd be moving tomorrow.

Amelia didn't show up the next morning at ten. By eleven, we were getting worried. She hadn't answered her phone either. "Maybe she changed her mind." Max went back to look out the front window.

"I doubt it," I said. "You just saw her yesterday, and she was really happy about your coming." I still didn't want Max to go, but I felt much better about it this morning. Max and I had a long talk, and she was all excited about the things we could do on the farm. All of her ideas included me, so I figured my worries about losing her as a friend had mostly been my imagination.

"Maybe we should drive out there," my mother suggested.

By now Max was pacing and looking worried. "Do you think something could have happened to her?"

"Let's hope not." Mom grabbed her keys from the hook on the wall.

After calling our neighbors and asking if Sam could stay for a while with the twins, Mom tossed me the keys and I hurried out to unlock the van and then got into the backseat. Max put her suitcases in the back and climbed into the backseat beside me. Mom was out the door and into the car before I got my seat belt on. "Okay, we're set. Carly said she'd watch Sam."

About halfway to the farm we saw Amelia's pickup sitting alongside the road with a flat tire. A tire jack and a spare tire were propped up next to the flat. "Looks like she tried to change the tire." Mom pulled up behind the truck and got out. Amelia was nowhere around. Getting back into the van, Mom said, "There are several possibilities. She may have gotten a ride into town."

"Wouldn't we have seen her?" I asked.

"Not necessarily."

"She could have walked back to the farm," Max suggested. "Maybe we should keep driving."

"Good call, Max." Mom eased back onto the road. "Her place is about two miles from here. I hope nothing has happened to her."

CHAPTER NINE

We found Amelia and Molly just as they were turning into the long driveway. Mom stopped and leaned out the window. "Hello. Looks like you had some trouble back there."

Amelia took off her wide-brimmed hat and wiped her brow with the hanky that she pulled out of her pants pocket. Her damp grey hair was matted and sticking to her head where the hatband had been. She had on a white blouse and khaki shorts. Her long tan legs looked like they belonged to someone my mother's age.

"Unfortunately, yes," she said. "Today is one of those rare times I wish I had a cell phone so I could have called you. My son has been after me to get one for several years now. Maybe I'll reconsider."

"They are nice—especially if you have an emergency," Mom agreed. "Well, hop in, and we'll give you a ride to the house."

She climbed into the front seat. "I suppose I should have waited for someone to come along," Amelia said, "but I'm not very good at sitting around. Especially on a day like today. Gets mighty hot in that pickup." She set her hat on her legs. "Ah, this air conditioning feels wonderful."

"I'm glad you're okay," Max said.

"Thank you. I feel terrible about keeping you waiting. This shouldn't have happened. The tires are fairly new, so I can't imagine why one of them would go flat. And those lug nuts were impossible to get off."

"Maybe you ran over a nail or something," I said.

"I suppose that's possible. I'll call Randy at the service station. He'll drive out and fix it for me. Perhaps you can give me a ride back to the pickup—after we have some iced tea." She glanced back at us and smiled. "I made some more of those cookies this morning."

The moment we got inside, Amelia headed for the phone to call Randy, who not only agreed to change the tire, but said he'd bring a friend and would drive the pickup back to the farm.

"Is this all you have?" Mrs. Truesdale asked when Max brought in her two suitcases.

"There's a box of stuff at the Miller place. We can get that later."

"Why don't you girls go upstairs and start unpacking while I make some lunch?"

Mom protested. "Amelia, let me make lunch. You should be resting after that hike."

Amelia laughed and said, "My goodness, that was only two miles. I walk more than that just working the farm every day."

"Well, at least let me help you." Mom followed Amelia into the kitchen while I followed Max up the stairs. Max is pretty strong, but it still took a lot of oomph to drag her suitcases up the stairs. She opened the bags, then looked in the closet and the chest of drawers. "There's way more room in here than I need. Maybe you could keep some clothes here so you wouldn't have to pack a bag every time."

"Sure." I liked the idea. It would almost be like sharing a room.

She set a worn-out, scruffy bear on the bedside stand and slid a book with a cloth cover and binding into the drawer.

"What's that?" I asked.

"My journal."

"You keep a journal? Like a diary?"

Max shrugged. "Sometimes I write in it. Heidi gave it to me. She said writing down my feelings could help me think things through."

"Does it help?" I had a journal, too, that I'd never show anyone —ever.

"I don't know. I haven't written in it that much. I started to, but haven't had all that much time. Maybe I will now."

Max had seemed quiet even before Amelia ended up being late. Maybe she was having second thoughts. "Are you glad you came here?"

Her shoulders rose and fell. "Don't know. Mrs. T is a lot tougher than I thought she would be." She smiled. "Can you believe her walking two miles? My aunt complained if she had to walk out to the mailbox."

"I like Amelia," I said, thinking that she and Max might be a good match after all.

"Me too." Max took an armful of clothes to the closet and dumped them on the floor, then started putting them on hangers. They were all wrinkled, as Max hadn't taken time to fold any of them before putting them in the suitcase. I tended to be neat and tidy with almost everything. I offered to fold the clothes for her, but she said my way was too slow. I ignored her and hung up a shirt. It and two others on the pile must have been the ones Mom bought. So far I hadn't seen Max wear them, and I wondered why. Maybe because they were like the kind of tops I'd seen some of the girls at school wearing. There was a skirt and a pair of jeans on the pile too. "Did you go shopping with my mom?"

She eyed the knit top and nodded. "They make me feel weird—like I'm conforming. Don't tell her though."

"She'll know if you don't ever wear them."

"Did you hear what Mrs. T said about her tires?" Max asked, changing the subject.

"You mean that they were new?" I took down a hanger and grabbed up a pair of wrinkled cargo pants. After hanging them up, I smoothed some of the wrinkles out with my hands.

"Yeah. What if someone punctured it?"

I frowned. "Who would do that?"

"Vandals, maybe." Max frowned. "I'm not saying it happened. I'm just thinking that with all the trouble she's been having, this might be part of a plan to make things hard for her."

"And if things get too hard, she might be forced to sell."

"Right."

I suggested that when we had some time, maybe later that night, we could list what we knew had happened so far. Maybe we were worrying over nothing, but I had a feeling Mrs. Truesdale might be in more trouble than we first thought.

We had most of the clothes put away by the time Mom called us down for lunch. They had made sandwiches and had set a bowl of chips on the table with a big pitcher of tea.

Lunch was going great until we heard a knock on the door and a man barged in without waiting for anyone to answer. Molly came up behind him, wagging her tail as if she was waiting for him to pet her. The man had brown hair that was gray at the temples. He peered at us through his round black-framed glasses. With dark slacks and a dress shirt and tie, he looked like a businessman. His eyes were blue—just a shade darker than Amelia's. The reason I noticed was because they were staring straight at me.

"Freddy!" Mrs. Truesdale set her cloth napkin on her plate and stood up. "What on earth are you doing here? It's the middle of the week."

"Mother, have you lost your mind? You bring a stranger into the house without consulting me. A delinquent teenager no less." His angry gaze slid from me to Max and back again like he was trying to figure out which kid was the delinquent.

I swallowed hard. Freddy must be Amelia's son. Would he make Max leave? Could he? Max and I looked at each other, and I could tell she was wondering the same thing.

"We were having lunch, dear." Amelia acted like she hadn't heard him. "Would you like to join us?"

"No, I won't *join* you." He hit the countertop with his fist.

"Well, then, perhaps you'd like to have a seat in the living room while my guests and I eat lunch. This is Max, by the way." She placed a hand on Max's shoulder and gave it a slight squeeze as if to tell Max not to worry. "And you remember Amy Miller and her daughter, Jessie."

"Hello, Fred," Mom said. "It's nice to see you again." I could tell Mom didn't mean it. She was being polite, and I wasn't sure why. The guy was rude. When Amelia introduced me, I turned away to take a bite of the cucumber-and-cream-cheese sandwich.

Fred stared at my mother for a second and seemed to relax a little. He actually smiled. "I do remember you. In fact, I have two of your paintings in my home and one in my office." He pulled out a chair and sat down. "I apologize for the interruption."

"You seem upset." Mom picked up her iced tea and took a sip.

"I am, actually. I got a call this morning from a . . . a friend telling me what my mother was up to." He stole a glance at Amelia.

"What I'm up to is no concern of yours or your friend's." Mrs. Truesdale went over to the cupboard to get a place setting.

"But taking in a foster child at your age is insane."

"It's a wonderful idea." She set a plate in front of him and poured him some tea. Smiling at Max, she said, "It will be fun having a youngster around again."

"But you're . . ."

"Too old? My goodness, Fred. You're the one who tells me I shouldn't be living out here alone. I'd think you'd be happy about Max coming to live with me."

He didn't comment, but I had the feeling he wasn't giving up either. He'd called Max a delinquent. I wondered where he'd gotten his information.

I felt bad for Max and wished there was something I could do. I started talking about the adventure we'd had yesterday when Max and I had heard Amelia scream and had come to rescue her.

Amelia's laugh seemed nervous. "Not that I needed rescuing, but it gave me a chance to get to know these two young ladies better."

Freddy didn't say anything, but I don't think my storytelling helped Max's cause any. He kept looking at my head, then Max's. I was used to people staring at my bald head. Sometimes I told them about the chemo treatments and sometimes I didn't. I decided to tell Freddy. "I have leukemia," I said. "My hair didn't grow back."

"And my aunt shaved my head because she thought I told the police she was on drugs." Max stared back at him as if daring him to make a comment.

Amelia winced. I don't think she wanted her son to know that Max had been abused or that her guardians had been drug users. "But that's all over now," she said, taking hold of Max's hand. "You'll be safe here."

"But will *you*?" Freddy pursed his lips. "How well do you know this girl? And with a history of drug use . . ."

That was it. I stood up and curled my fists into balls. "Max does not use drugs. You don't know her at all. She's one of the nicest people I've ever met and she's my friend. You should be ashamed of yourself coming in here and acting rude and . . . and . . ." I couldn't think of the word.

All of a sudden I felt stupid. My stomach hurt and I felt all shaky inside like when you haven't eaten for too long or when you have to get up in front of the whole class and give a report. Mom put her arm around my waist and motioned for me to sit down. I did.

"Obnoxious." Mrs. Truesdale finished the sentence for me. "Jessie is right, Fred. You don't know Max, and you are being extremely rude. In fact, unless you change your tone, young man, I'm going to have to ask you to leave."

"Fine." He glared at his mother and pushed back his chair. Throwing his napkin down on the untouched plate, he said, "We'll talk later. And don't think this is over. I'm going into town to talk with someone who'll listen to reason."

He left, slamming the door behind him. Poor Molly stood there watching him and whimpering. She looked back at us with soulful eyes and sat back down in front of the door.

Amelia smiled at us, but her eyes looked sad. "I hope you won't let Freddy's tirade upset your lunch. He tends to be a bit overprotective where I'm concerned." She went to the counter and brought back a plate of her lavender shortbread cookies.

"These are wonderful, Amelia," my mother said. "The girls and I were talking yesterday and decided you should go nationwide with them."

"Oh, thank you, but I don't think so."

I took one, but didn't feel like eating. I knew Fred could make trouble for Max, and I didn't feel comfortable leaving her here alone. What if Fred came back and hurt Max or something? I'd managed to help her to escape one abusive situation, and I didn't want her to end up in another one. Although I trusted Amelia, I did not trust her son.

I wasn't sure what Max was thinking, but I knew I didn't want to leave her. "You need to get your bike," I said, remembering it was still at our house.

"I know," Max said. "I could drive back with you and ride my bike back out here. It isn't that far."

"It's too hot." Mom glanced at Amelia. "I'll bring you back, Max. That's not a problem."

"Would it be okay if Jessie spent the night?" Max asked.

"Really?" I hoped Amelia would say yes.

"Of course," she said. "I'd be delighted."

Max seemed relieved. I figured she wasn't too thrilled about the possibility of another encounter with Fred either.

Mom settled a hand on my shoulder. "I'm not sure about your staying all night, Jessie. We'll need to check with your father."

"But . . ."

She gave me a no-arguments look. "You've only been home for twenty-four hours. We'll see what Dad says."

I blew out a long breath. Mom tended to be overprotective at times. I didnt know if she wanted to make sure I didn't overdo it or if she wanted to protect me from Fred.

We piled into the van, promising Amelia we'd have Max back in an hour. Just as Mom started the car, a man drove in with Amelia's pickup, followed by Randy's tow truck. Randy jumped out and handed Amelia the keys. "Here you go, ma'am."

"Thanks. What do I owe you?"

"Nothing. Unless you want to give me some of that scone mix you make."

"Consider it done." Amelia nodded toward the pickup. "Did you figure out what the problem was?"

"Sure did. There was a slice in the tire. Looks like someone cut it."

"Cut it? I don't understand."

"I don't know what to tell you." He held out his open palms. "Vandals, I'd imagine. The cut caused a slow leak, so it might have happened when you were in town yesterday or sometime during the night."

Amelia sucked in a deep breath. "Thank you, Randy. I don't have any of the scone packages on hand right now, but I'll bring some next time I come into town."

When the men left, I glanced over at Max, who looked more than a little worried. Something weird was going on here.

CHAPTER TEN

I ended up getting to stay over with Max, but mainly because Dad said so. I could tell he was worried about me, but Dad is into the whole deal about treating me like a normal kid whenever possible. I really wanted to go, and with Max and me both pleading, he finally caved. Mom did too, but told me to make sure I had a cell phone. I was to call them if Fred showed up and caused any trouble. If he did, Dad would come out. To be honest, I was more worried about whoever had slashed Amelia's tire, but I didn't say so.

The whole family came along to drop Max and me off at the farm.

"I want to see the goat that butted Mrs. Truesdale," Sam insisted once we were in the van.

I laughed. "You'd better be careful, or he'll butt you too."

"She's right, Sam," Dad said. "Goats can be rascals."

"Will you ride me on your shoulders, Dad?" he asked after thinking on it.

"Sure, Son." Dad winked at me in the rearview mirror.

Once I got my stuff set in Max's room, we went outside to

where Sam was feeding the goat. Amelia had put him in a pen. "He loves attention and he's usually very sweet. But he's frisky."

"What's his name?" Sam reached into the pen and patted his head.

"He's a Nubian," she said. "And not being very original with names, I call him Nubie."

We played with the goat for a few minutes while Amelia showed my parents around. She insisted we all stay for dinner, so we did. We ate outside on the deck facing the lake. The gentle slope down to the water reminded me of our house. She'd made a pot roast and acted like she'd planned for a lot of people. Maybe she had. Amelia may have been old, but she sure could get around. I just never knew how well until these last couple of days. Still, I was worried about her. I wondered how far her son would go to get her off the farm and into a place in town. Maybe Max and I could talk to her more about that tonight.

My parents and Sam left around seven thirty. When they'd gone, Amelia suggested we relax in the living room with some tea. I had just finished mine when Amelia said, "I have a project I need to finish up tonight. Would you girls like to help?"

"Sure. What is it?" Max asked.

"Lavender sachets. Why don't you two come with me and we'll set up in the kitchen." We followed Amelia into the craft room where she had stacks and stacks of material. She opened a closet and brought out a plastic container filled with all sorts of pretty sachets, then handed the box to Max. "You take these; and Jessie, if you'd carry my sewing supplies, I'll bring the lavender."

Minutes later, we were all sitting at the kitchen table. She used a funnel to fill the sachets with dried lavender that had been infused with a special oil to make the scent last. After showing us how, she handed that job to us. I held the funnel while Max spooned in the lavender. As we filled them, Amelia sewed up the small opening in each bag.

We worked like that for about an hour. Even with thick cushions on the chair, I was getting a sore behind and my muscles hurt. I leaned my head back and closed my eyes for a minute.

"You're not falling asleep on us, are you?" Max asked.

"No. Just resting for a second."

Amelia set her sewing aside. "I don't know about you girls, but I'm getting rather tired."

Looking over the finished sachets, Max whistled. "We must have done fifty of these things."

"Sixty actually." Amelia removed her glasses. "Well done, girls. I may have to consider hiring you."

"It was fun." I'd never been much into crafty things, but working alongside Max and Amelia had made the time go by fast. The sachets were beautiful.

"I don't know how you girls feel about bedtime, but I'm an early riser. I'll be heading for bed now and will be up around 4:30 or 5:00—or when the sun gets me up." She smiled. "If you want to stay up longer or get up later, I'll try not to wake you."

I looked at Max, who seemed deep in thought. "I'm with you,

Mrs. T," she finally said. "I've never gotten up that early, but I'll get used to it."

I was surprised by Max's answer. Her aunt and uncle stayed awake most of the night and didn't get up before noon unless they had to go to work. When I asked her about it after we'd gone to bed, she said her real parents had been like Mrs. T, going to bed around ten and getting up at six. "I never did get used to going to bed late. I like getting up early."

I yawned. "That's good." I closed my eyes and must have fallen asleep right away cause I don't remember anything else until Max woke me up around 1:00 a.m.

"Jess! Did you hear that?" She shook my shoulder.

"What?" I sat up and rubbed my eyes. The room was dark except for the yard lights filtering through the blinds.

"Shh. Listen." Max pointed toward the ceiling. "Somebody's up in the attic."

It was quiet for a moment, and then I heard a soft shuffling noise. "It's probably just a mouse."

"That's no mouse. I heard footsteps."

I sat up straighter. I heard them too now, along with what sounded like the click of a door closing. "Maybe it's Amelia," I whispered, hoping that was the case. I sure didn't like the alternative.

"I'll go check." Max was about to open the door when we heard a creak on the floorboard in the hall. The mystery person was right outside the door. I shook my head and motioned for her to stop. Fortunately she did.

I joined her at the door and whispered, "I can hear the steps creaking."

Max eased open the door, peeked out, and ducked back in. "It's definitely not Mrs. T. We need to call the police."

"There's no phone in here," I moaned. I'd left my cell phone downstairs in my sweatshirt pocket.

"Did you notice if there was one in Mrs. T's bedroom?"

I shook my head. "I only saw the one downstairs in the kitchen, and I'm not going down there."

"He's probably gone by now." Max ran to the window. "I don't see a car. Jess, come here, quick. That's him. He's heading for the lake."

Sure enough, a large, dark figure was running toward the dock. "He's carrying something." The intruder placed a package on the seat of his boat and began rowing away. Max ran for the door. "We need to tell Mrs. T."

My thoughts, exactly.

CHAPTER ELEVEN

Amelia had a phone in her bedroom, on the nightstand beside her bed. She put her hearing aids in and listened as we told her what we had heard and seen, then called 911.

"My goodness," she said as she hung up. "What a terrible thing to have happen, and on your first night here." She grabbed her robe from the end of her bed and slipped it on. "Let's go downstairs and have some chamomile tea. That should settle us down. I'm just glad no one was hurt." She frowned. "Though I can't imagine what a thief would have been doing in the attic of all places. Are you sure he was up there?"

"Positive," Max said. "We heard him. I think he might have dropped something, because the noise woke me up."

"Well, I didn't hear a thing." She chuckled. "Course, I'm half deaf without my hearing aids."

We sipped on our tea and talked about crime scenes and how you don't touch anything. We all wanted to go up in the attic to see what the thief had taken, but wouldn't. We didn't want to contaminate the crime scene.

A sheriff's patrol car pulled into the driveway. Fifteen minutes from the time of the call—I was impressed.

The deputy, Jack Keagan, is a friend of my dad's. They went to school together, and his daughter, Hope, is in my class. She's one of the girls who don't talk to me or Max. Jack's okay though. He was one of the guys who tried to find me when I got lost on the lake.

"Hello, Jessie, Max. What are you two doing out here?" Before either of us could answer he added, "Amelia, are these two girls giving you trouble?"

"Certainly not," Mrs. Truesdale said. "In fact, quite the opposite. Max is my foster daughter, or she will be as soon as we complete the paperwork. Jessie is our guest."

He looked like he didn't believe her. "You called about a break-in?"

While Max and Mrs. T talked to Deputy Keagan, I thought about the guy we'd seen get into the boat. At least we thought it was a guy. I suppose it could have been a woman. There was something about that walk and the size that made me think it was a man.

When they finished talking, the deputy went outside and looked around. Several minutes later, he came back in and asked Amelia to go with him to look through the house for anything that might be missing.

"You were right, Max," Amelia said when they came back into the kitchen. "Our intruder dropped a jar full of buttons. That must have been what woke you. They're all over the floor. It's a wonder he didn't fall on them."

"Is there anything missing?" I asked.

"Nothing that I could see. It's hard to know, as I don't get up there all that often. The lid on my old trunk was up. I'm sure it was down before." She sighed. "I'll have to have a look around tomorrow when the light is better."

"Did you get any prints?" Max asked the deputy.

"Nope." He shook his head. "Just took a quick look around. Made sure there weren't any intruders. I could send a crime scene specialist out here, but it doesn't look like your thief got away with anything important. Besides, the guy was probably wearing gloves."

Max rolled her eyes. "There was a man in Mrs. T's house. Isn't that important? What if he was casing the joint? What if he plans to come back and murder us?"

"I doubt that's the case, Max." Amelia turned to the deputy. "She's right, you know. He could come back. I think maybe you should send someone out. If there's any possibility . . ."

"How did he get in?" I asked.

"There was no sign of a break-in." Jack rubbed a hand through his hair like he was annoyed with me for asking. "Which means the guy may have had a key, or he may have climbed in through an open window."

"Oh, I never leave the windows on the main floor unlocked."

"Maybe he used a ladder and came in through one of the upstairs windows." His tone softened. "Mrs. Truesdale, did you see or hear anyone?"

"No, but the girls told me . . ."

"Maybe the girls thought they saw something. You know how kids are. Maybe they were sneaking around in the attic and dropped the jar, then made up the story."

"We were not in the attic," Max insisted. "And we did not make this up."

"We didn't," I said. "We both heard him and we saw him get into his boat. He had something in his hands."

She nodded. "I believe you." To the deputy she said, "I'd like you to leave now, Jack. I'll call the sheriff if I have to, but I want that CSI person out here as soon as possible."

"I'll talk to the sheriff myself, ma'am. He'll have to okay the crime scene investigation." Jack shook his head. "And frankly, I don't think he'll see much point either."

Amelia didn't like his response. "You tell Howard he'd better have someone out here in the morning or he'll not be getting my vote come election time. He won't be getting a lot of votes if I have to tell people how uninterested his deputy was about a break-in."

I almost felt sorry for Deputy Keagan, but he deserved it. He shouldn't have been brushing it off, or worse, trying to blame Max and me.

"I'll see what I can do, ma'am. But with summer here, we're shorthanded. You know how it is."

"I know. All I'm asking is that you take this seriously."

Jack Keagan eyed Max and me. "Oh, we will." He started to leave then, and my stomach got all queasy. At the door he looked back at us. "You have a dog, don't you?"

"Yes, why?"

"Doesn't she usually bark when people come around?"

"Yes."

He nodded as if he'd just proved his point and left.

"He thinks we did it and made up the story," Max said. "Well, we didn't. You believe us, don't you, Mrs. T?"

"Of course I do." She said the words with conviction, but I thought I saw a flicker of doubt in her eyes. "Why don't we all go back to bed? Let's see if we can get a few more hours of sleep before sunup."

Max didn't say much when we got back to bed, but I could tell she was worried. Maybe she'd noticed the same hesitation in Amelia's eyes that I had. Not that I blamed Amelia for doubting us. Deputy Keagan had a point. Where was Molly and why hadn't she barked? Come to think about it, she hadn't barked when the deputy came either. Of course, Molly, might have known both men. She didn't bark when Fred came. I made a mental note to talk to Amelia about that possibility in the morning.

I was worried about the break-in, but something else too. If Amelia didn't believe us, she'd probably change her mind about Max living with her. Max already had a reputation for being a troublemaker, and Fred Truesdale had called her a delinquent. Would Amelia change her mind?

I'd like to have Max come back and live with us, but not because she had to. Max is a totally honest person, and it made me furious to see people accuse her of being a delinquent, a thief, or a liar. Unfortunately, I had no idea what to do about it.

CHAPTER TWELVE

Waking up early wasn't as hard as I thought it would be. I lay there for a while enjoying the quiet and letting the scent of something yummy drift into my nostrils. Max was already up and had made her bed. I heard a dog barking and wondered again why Molly hadn't barked last night. That thought got me out of bed and into my clothes in under two minutes.

Molly met me at the foot of the stairs and sniffed at my bare feet. I sat down on the second step from the bottom and petted her black-and-white head. When my hand touched the left side of her head, she yelped and pulled away. "Did that hurt?" I gently touched the tender spot again and felt a lump. "What happened?" I stroked the silky hairs along her throat.

"Good morning, sleepyhead." Amelia stood in the kitchen doorway, wiping her hands on a towel. "I see you've discovered Molly's injury."

"That must be why she didn't bark last night."

"It's a good guess."

"Poor Molly." I leaned back when she tried to lick my face.

"She was lying on the front porch this morning, crying and wanting in. Her hair was matted and bloody. I cleaned her up. She seems all right now, but I'll call the vet as soon as the office opens."

I bit my lower lip. "Who would want to hurt Molly?"

"No one that I know of." She tipped her head to assess the Australian shepherd. "She may have been hit by a car."

"Or maybe it was the burglar."

"True. Either way, we know why your intruder came and went with no complaints from Molly."

"Where's Max?" I asked.

"Gathering eggs for our breakfast. Are you ready to eat?"

"I'm starved." I washed my hands in the sink and took a seat at the table just as Max came in. "Something sure smells good," I said. "What are you making?"

"Scones," Max announced, setting her basket on the counter. "I made them this morning. There's bacon in the oven."

"I didn't know you could cook."

"Sure. I learned real fast after I moved in with Bob and Serena." She lifted her shoulders in a deep sigh. "I had to either learn how to cook or starve to death."

We'd been friends for around five months, and there were still a lot of things I didn't know about Max. It made me sad to think about how Max had been treated. I guess I'd never thought about her not having enough to eat. My mom and dad always made meals. I'd learned how to make a few things, but only because I wanted to, like Jell-O and the kind of cookies you buy already made so all you have to do is cut them up and put them in the oven to bake.

"I got six eggs," Max told Amelia as she washed her hands. "There are more out there, but one of the hens wouldn't let me come near her."

Amelia chuckled. "That would be Elvira. She's my best layer, but she thinks all of her eggs are fertilized and she's very protective. I have some special feed I use to get her off the nest, and I leave two plastic eggs in her nest all the time so she doesn't get too upset. Personally, I think she was traumatized at some time in her life. She's a bit loony."

"Have your hens ever had baby chicks?" I asked.

"Occasionally, when I need more layers."

The timer on the oven beeped, and Max took out her scones.

"Lavender?" I asked.

She giggled. "No, chocolate chip and hazelnut."

"Yum."

Max put the scones on a plate and I set the table while Mrs. T scrambled the eggs with a little cream and cheese. She put in some crumbled bacon, onion, and mushrooms so it was like an omelet only all mushed up. Max put milk and orange juice on the table, and we all sat down. Amelia asked me to say the blessing. Even though I said grace a lot at home, I was kind of embarrassed doing it in front of Max and Amelia. "Lord, thank You for this food, and thank You that Molly is okay. And please help us find whoever was in the house last night. Oh, and keep us safe. Amen."

"Thank you, Jessie." Amelia smiled at me. I think she knew that Max wasn't much interested in church stuff. Max was used to saying grace though, because she'd been at my house so often.

When we finished eating, I offered to do the dishes.

"I'd appreciate that," Amelia said. "I'm going to finish up those sachets we worked on last night. I need to run them into the tea shop today."

"Can I help?" Max asked.

"Of course. Why don't you and Jessie clear the table while I bring them out?"

I was running water in the sink when Amelia made a sound like a puppy yelping.

Max ran to the craft room. I dried my hands and hurried after her. Amelia sank into a chair. "All that work . . . and . . . they're ruined."

Max stood there with her mouth open. She looked over at me. "The guy from last night must have done this."

"What?" I came closer. "Oh, no." The bags had been slashed, the lavendar spilling out of open wounds.

CHAPTER THIRTEEN

"What a cruel thing to do." Amelia took a hanky out of her pocket and dabbed at her watery eyes.

I was more angry than sad. "It must have been the burglar."

"But why would he destroy the sachets?" Max knelt down and fingered one of them. "This doesn't make any sense."

Amelia leaned forward and rested her head in her hands. "It will take me days to replace these, and that's if I can find the time to work on them. I'll have to call Janet Cavanaugh and tell her I can't fill the order."

Teeth clenched, Max set the box on the floor and began pawing through it. "Here's a good one." She held up a deep red velvet heart with lace ribbon trim. "Here's one more." She found eleven in all that hadn't been slashed and several that Amelia thought could be fixed.

"I suppose that's something." Amelia thanked Max for going through them. "But I still need forty more."

"We could help you fix these and make some new ones," Max said. "Just show us what to do."

"Oh, I couldn't ask . . ."

"Please." Max started dumping the herbs out of the damaged sachets.

Mrs. Truesdale smiled and nodded. "All right." Standing, she said, "Max, set the ones that could be mended on the sewing machine table. We'll form an assembly line. Jessie, as soon as you've finished the dishes I'll put you to work stuffing the sachets."

I did the dishes (something I often had to do at home), cleaned off the kitchen table, and then hurried into the craft room where Max was cutting out shapes and Amelia was sewing them together. They already had a pile waiting for me to stuff. Since stuffing them went faster than sewing them, I asked if I could close the little opening I'd funneled the lavender into. Amelia showed me how. By noon we had made sixty-five—more than enough for the tea shop and some extras to put out at the roadside stand.

Mom called, wanting to know when I'd be home. I told her what had happened, and she said I could stay as long as I didn't overdo. Max and I offered to watch the stand at the end of the driveway while Amelia ran her errands in town. She needed to take Molly in to the vet, take the sachets and some lavender short-bread cookies to the tea shop, and take Randy his scone mix.

We rode with Amelia in her pickup to the end of the driveway, and Molly rode in the back. Amelia got out and started to open the stand to let us in. The door was ajar. She held a hand out for us to stay back and pushed open the door. "Oh, my," she cried, as she pulled on a cord, filling the stand with light. "It looks like he was in here too."

The shelves were empty and the floor was covered with glass, scone mix, crumbs and jams, and torn packages.

"Why would anyone do this?" Her voice was soft and tearful. She didn't cry though. "It's as though someone is trying to ruin my business, or at the very least discourage me."

I thought about Fred wanting her to sell the place.

Max frowned. "We have to find out who was at the house last night."

Max and I had made our way into the stand. I backed out when glass shards from a broken bottle of jam crunched under my shoe. "We should call the sheriff again. Deputy Keagan needs to see this. There must be some clues here."

Amelia shook her head and rubbed her forehead. "There's no point. Besides, I think I may know who's behind this, but I had no idea he'd go to such extremes to get me to retire."

Max frowned. "You mean Fred?"

She closed her eyes and nodded. "I hate to think that he could do something so destructive, but who else could it be? Deputy Keagan said he didn't see any sign of a break-in. Freddy has a key, of course. And he was terribly angry with me."

"No matter how mad I got with my parents, I would never ruin their things. It would be like me slashing my mother's paintings. Doesn't he love you?"

Amelia's shoulders slumped. "I . . . I'm sure he does."

"Not a great way to show it," Max said.

Amelia sighed. "He wants what's best for me. Maybe he thinks this will force me to give up the farm. Without my business, I can't afford to stay here."

"I'm sorry." Amelia looked so sad, I hugged her. Now that she'd said that it might be Fred, I was having a hard time believing that her own son could be that cruel. "Maybe it wasn't him. He might be mad at you, but do you really think he'd hurt Molly and ruin all of this? He'd have to be a terrible man. Besides," I reasoned, "if it was him, he wouldn't have had to hurt Molly. She didn't bark when he came in yesterday."

"You know, you're right, Jessie." Amelia stepped back and squeezed my shoulders. "Freddy could have come and gone as he pleased. And you're right—he'd never hurt Molly."

"Can you think of anybody else who'd do something like this?" I asked. "Do you have any enemies?"

"No . . . at least none that I know of."

Max folded her arms and stood there with her legs slightly apart. "You can't give up, Mrs. T. You can't let this . . . this terrorist stop you."

She smiled at that, but her eyes were still sad. "I can't imagine Freddy deliberately ruining my business. He just wants me in a retirement home where I'll be safe. Maybe it's time I did as he asked. I certainly don't have the energy for this."

"But if you did that, what would happen to Max?" I asked. "You said you wanted to be her foster mom."

"Forget it, Jess." Max stepped out into the sunshine. "It's no big deal. I'll just stay with you."

But it was a big deal to Max. Her eyes told me that much. She already felt like a reject, and having Amelia change her mind would make her feel worse.

Amelia looked at Max, then at me, and after what seemed like a long time, she said, "You are absolutely right, girls. I have always been and still am a strong woman. The good Lord has helped me weather all sorts of storms, many of them much worse than this."

She stepped outside and pulled the door closed behind her. "Come on. Get back in the pickup. We're going to make our deliveries, and then we'll stop at the sheriff's office. And after that we'll come back here and clean up this mess."

"All right!" Max gave me a high five and we piled into the cab and headed for town.

We stopped by the veterinarian's office where the vet told Amelia that Molly had a mild concussion and to keep an eye on her. The next stop was the tea shop, where we told Janet Cavanaugh what had happened. After that we stopped at the sheriff's office.

"We'll check it out, Amelia," Sheriff Clark said, "but it was probably vandals. Most likely that group of teenagers camping out at the Alpine Village. They're celebrating graduation. Though if they're not careful, some of them will end up in jail instead of college." He laughed.

I didn't think it was funny. Kids got blamed for everything— especially tourists who were teenagers. At least he hadn't implied that Max and I were responsible like Jack Keagan had.

"Nonsense," Amelia said. "What reason would they have?"

"Those rabble-rousers don't need a reason." The sheriff made a few notes in a small pad.

"Well, whoever it was knocked out Molly and got into the house. Your deputy didn't even bother taking prints."

"He told me about it. There's not much use in doing that. Like he said, the intruder was probably wearing gloves. From what I understand, no one was hurt and nothing is missing."

"This is pointless." Amelia herded us to the door. "Let's go clean up the mess, girls."

"I have my deputies checking on the break-in, Amelia. We'll let you know if we find anything."

"Well, that's something."

I wondered if the sheriff's department would even look for the guy. Amelia still hadn't gone up in the attic to see if there was something missing. Maybe there'd be time this afternoon. I'd have to remind her. It seemed to me that if we found out what the guy had taken, we might have some idea who he might be. I thought again about Fred and decided he wouldn't have any reason to break into the house to take something. All he had to do was ask Amelia.

By the time we got back to the farm there were four cars in the driveway, one of them our van. My mom was leaning against it talking to Janet Cavanaugh and two other ladies from our church. Molly barked at them. "It's all right, Molly," Amelia said. "They're friends." Molly jumped out of the pickup bed and went to sniff at them.

"Are you girls having a party and didn't invite me?" Amelia slid out of the cab and closed the door.

Janet Cavanaugh came toward us. "When you told me what happened I called around to get some volunteers. I left Ivy in charge of the shop and picked up Elsie and Marcia."

"We're having a party all right," Mom said. "A cleaning party. Bring on the mess."

Amelia's lower lip quivered, and this time she actually got tears in her eyes. The women each hugged her. Mom hugged me and Max. "I think it's wonderful how you girls helped Amelia make sachets this morning. I'm so proud of you."

I felt proud of us too, and even prouder when we all pitched in to work on the roadside stand. Amelia opened the front panel of the stand, letting in the daylight.

We salvaged what we could from the mess, which wasn't much. Amelia said she'd just close the stand for a few days until she could replenish her inventory.

When we'd finished, Amelia invited everyone up to the house for coffee, tea, and snacks. After eating, Mom told me I needed to go home with her so I could get some rest. "You have dark lines under your eyes, Jessie. You must be exhausted."

I protested a little, but knew there wasn't much point. Besides, I was too tired to put up much of a fight. We said good-bye and left. Once home I took my quilt and pillow out on the swing, and for a total of about two minutes, I lay there wondering who had been in Amelia's attic and why. One thing I knew for sure—it wasn't vandals.

It still upset me that Deputy Keagan could insinuate that Max and I had something to do with it. "We'll just have to prove him wrong," I murmured as I closed my eyes.

CHAPTER FOURTEEN

The next morning I stayed in bed for a long time, waiting for my body to cooperate with my mind. I wanted to get up, get dressed, and ride my bike out to the farm. Wishful thinking, I know. With the way I felt I'd probably make it as far as our driveway.

Mom brought me breakfast in bed and said I should rest. I didn't want to, but I didn't seem to have much choice. I was just too weak. Over the last two days I'd tried to do too much and was paying for it now. Around noon, I managed to get dressed and haul myself down to the lawn swing. I could hear Sam and the twins playing in their tree fort next door. Mom was humming a tune while she set up her paints and easel a few feet away from me.

"Hi, sweetie." She stopped singing when she heard me come out. "Feeling better?"

"A little." I dropped onto the swing and settled the quilt over me. "Mom?"

"Hmm?"

"Remember when we were driving home from the hospital? You said something about Mrs. Truesdale's son. You promised to tell me later, but I never got a chance to ask you about it."

"Well . . ." She squeezed some green paint onto her palette. "First of all, you need to know that Fred isn't a bad person. I don't share his point of view, but I understand why he feels the way he does."

"You mean about wanting his mother to move into a place for old people?"

"He wants his mother in a safe place. He's afraid that she'll fall or that something bad will happen to her. What he doesn't understand is that Amelia loves that farm and, for right now, at least, she's not in any imminent danger." Mom had already spread shades of blue and white over the canvas to create a sky. Pastel tans, browns, and greens made a background for the land. Now she dabbed on small strokes of green in the form of a tree.

"I just don't think trying to force her to give up the farm is a good idea."

"I don't either." I fluffed up my pillow. "Do you think he's the one who ruined all her stuff?"

"No." Mom seemed pretty definite. "Fred isn't that sort of person. And besides, why would he break into the house and rummage around in the attic?"

"I thought the same thing, but who else would it be?"

"I have no idea."

"Max said Carlos was gone."

She frowned. "Yes."

"Don't you think it's kind of strange that he'd leave without telling anyone?"

"Not really. I heard that he was living here illegally. Many of the migrant workers are."

The phone rang and Mom went inside to answer it. A few seconds later she came back out and handed the phone to me. "It's Max."

"Hi." I watched Mom go back to her painting and decided to go inside so I wouldn't disturb her.

"I'm coming into town to deliver some stuff. Do you want to meet me at the tea shop?" Max said.

"I'd like to, but I don't think I can ride my bike that far."

"Okay," she said. "I'll come to your place. I have to stop at the tea shop first, so give me an hour."

"Is everything okay?" I asked.

"Yeah, it's cool. No break-ins or anything. We made more sachets and cookies after you guys left. Molly stayed inside the house so we could hear her if she barked."

I felt better all of a sudden. Max sounded happy, and she was coming by to see me. Somehow she always managed to cheer me up.

Two hours passed and still no Max. I phoned out to the farm, but Amelia hadn't seen her. When I told Mom, she offered to drive me around to look for her. We stopped by the tea shop, but Janet Cavanaugh hadn't seen her. "Can we drive out to the farm?" I asked. "Maybe something happened on the way."

"I was about to suggest that." Mom chewed on her lip. She didn't say so, but I know she felt that Max had a little too much freedom.

"You don't think Mrs. Truesdale should have let her ride her bike into town alone?"

"No, honey, I don't. It's dangerous. There are so many predators out there these days. And it is summer. We have so many tourists."

As we drove, I watched along the side of the road. About halfway there, I spotted what looked like the tip of a wheel. "Stop."

Mom slammed on her brakes. "What is it?"

"I saw something back there on the other side of the road. Can you back up?"

Mom put the car in reverse, stopping where I said. We both got out of the car and hurried across the road.

"Max!" I screamed her name the minute I saw her. The bike lay in a twisted mess. The trailer she'd hooked onto the back of it to carry Amelia's orders was overturned in the muddy ditch. Max lay crumpled a few feet in front of the bike, smeared with mud and blood.

"What took you so long?" Max moaned as she tried to sit up.

"Don't try to move, Max," Mom said. "I'm calling for an ambulance."

Max put her head back down. "Somebody ran into me and drove away."

"Better send the sheriff too," Mom said into the phone. "Looks like a hit-and-run."

I couldn't believe what Max was telling us. I dropped to my knees at Max's side, wishing I could do something to help her. Mom crouched down beside me, the phone still open. "Can you tell if anything is broken?"

"My head. I flipped over the handlebars. Knocked me out for a while. My arm hurts."

"I'd better call Amelia." Mom punched the speed dial on her cell phone, and Amelia arrived in her pickup at the same time as the rescue truck and sheriff's deputy.

As it turned out, Max made it through the accident without too much damage. She had a gash on the head and one arm and lots of bruises, but nothing was broken. Mom and I sat in the waiting room at the hospital while the doctor stitched her up. Amelia insisted on being with Max the whole time.

While we waited, I thought about everything that had happened. First Amelia's slashed tire, then the break-in at the house and somebody trashing her sachets and the other things she'd made. Now someone had run Max off the road and totaled her bike. Someone was out to get Amelia Truesdale and didn't care who got hurt in the process. I wondered then if Carlos had really left town or if someone had forced him to leave, or worse. Maybe the person behind the burglary and vandalism had something to do with Carlos's disappearance. I thought about Martin, the person Amelia had hired to take Carlos's place, and realized I hadn't met him yet.

More than anything I wanted to get to the bottom of this crime spree, but what could I do? Right then an aide, dressed in blue scrubs, wheeled Max into the waiting room.

"We're ready to go." Amelia looked like she needed the wheelchair more than Max did. "Amy, do you think you could drive us back to my pickup?"

"Of course." Mom put in a call to Dad to let him know Max was okay and they were heading back to the farm.

Amelia sat up in front with Mom, and I crawled in back with Max. "What did the deputy say?" I asked once we'd gotten into our seat belts.

"There's some paint on the cart and my bike. They figure

someone's got some front-end damage. They'll try to find the person who did it."

"Did you see who hit you?"

Max looked down at her arm. "Sort of. I heard the engine and got a quick look before he hit me. All I saw was this old beat-up truck coming at me. I caught a glimpse of the driver, but I have no idea what he looks like."

"I can't imagine who would purposely do such a thing." Amelia glanced into the backseat. "I'm so sorry, Max. I think it might be best if we not go out alone. At least not until the sheriff can get to the bottom of this. In fact, I wouldn't blame you if you went back to live with the Millers. I'm suddenly dangerous to be around." She turned back to look at Mom. "I honestly can't come up with a reason for all this. It's as though someone has something against me."

"Max and I were talking about that after that guy broke into your house," I said. "What if someone wants to buy your farm? I mean, it's worth a lot of money, isn't it?"

"Yes." She frowned. "The realtor is an old friend. He's told me a number of times that I should consider selling. We've talked about it, but Charlie would never do anything like this. Besides, he owns a silver SUV."

I wasn't convinced of Charlie's innocence, but let it go.

"What about a developer?" I asked.

"She has a point, Amelia," Mom said. "Suppose someone contacted Charlie and discovered the property wasn't for sale. When did Charlie last talk to you about selling the farm?"

Way to go, Mom. I flashed a grin at Max.

Amelia rubbed at her forehead. "Several months ago. It's gotten to be a game with us. Every once in a while he'll call and ask if I'm ready to sell. I always say no." She shook her head. "I can't imagine anyone wanting my property badly enough to run down a 12-year-old girl."

"What about the new guy working for you?" Max asked.

"Martin? Not possible. He's been in Seattle for the last week. His mother has been ill. He's due back tomorrow."

Not impossible either, I thought. "Mom? Could I stay with Max tonight?" I didn't want Max to be alone. Not that I could do much if something happened, but I'd feel better if I could keep an eye on both Max and Amelia. Besides, I had a plan and needed Max to help me.

Mom glanced at Amelia. "I don't know, Jessie."

"Please."

"It's fine with me," Amelia said. "But we'd better ask Max if she's up to having a visitor."

Please, please, please. I offered a silent plea. When I stole a look at Max, my stomach took a tumble. I knew what she was going to say before she said it.

"Not a good idea, Jess. I need to rest. Maybe tomorrow."

She had a distant look in her eyes like she might be planning something without me. Maybe she was still in shock from the accident.

"Max is right, Jessie," Mom said. "You should both take it easy." We stopped at Amelia's pickup. The bike and cart, along with its contents, were gone—probably at the sheriff's office or the impound lot where the cops went through stuff looking for evidence. A hit-and-run was a crime, and this obviously wasn't Max's fault. They had to investigate this one.

Max got out of our car to ride with Amelia. "I'll call you tomorrow." She looked sleepy, probably from the pain pills the doctor had given her.

Disappointment hung around my shoulders while Mom and I drove back to our house. I didn't know whether to be mad or worried or just plain hurt. Our friendship should have been more solid, but with Max I never knew what to expect.

Mom pulled in the driveway and stopped the car, then gave me a worried look. "I'm going to get your brother. I'd like you to lie down."

I nodded. No use in arguing. Besides, I could hardly keep my eyes open. I hated being such a wimp. Maybe that's why Max hadn't wanted me to stay. She was like a parent sometimes, thinking I shouldn't try to do too much. That I might get sick again.

Tears pricked my eyes. I was feeling sorry for myself again. I hated when that happened. It's just that sometimes I'd give anything to be strong and healthy. Brushing away the tears with my sleeve, I headed for the back porch and fell asleep before I even had a chance to think about the trouble Mrs. Truesdale and Max were having. I don't remember much about the rest of the evening. I think I ate dinner before my dad carried me up to bed.

I didn't wake up until 10:30 the next morning. Yawning, I slipped my feet into my slippers and put one of Dad's hooded sweatshirts on over my pajamas. The sun was shining and I felt almost normal. I looked in the bathroom mirror, glad to see that the dark circles under my eyes had almost disappeared.

"Hey, sleepyhead." Mom gave me a hug and planted a kiss on the top of my bald head before taking a protein drink out of the fridge and setting it on the counter. She'd probably made it earlier. I had to drink at least one of them a day to build myself up.

I hitched myself onto the swivel bar stool and took a sip. Mmm, raspberry.

"What would you like for breakfast this morning?" Mom asked. "I have some blueberry pecan waffles left and some Canadian bacon I could heat up for you."

"That sounds good." I was actually hungry. Probably because I hadn't eaten much for dinner. "Did Max call?"

"Not yet. I suspect she slept in too. She had quite a day yesterday."

I nodded. "Hope she's okay."

"I imagine she'll be sore, but she's one lucky girl." Mom set a waffle and two pieces of bacon on a plate and put them in the microwave.

I thought about calling Max, but decided against it. She needed her sleep like I had needed mine. Sam came in from out-side and leaned up against me. I ruffled his thick dark hair, feeling a burst of jealousy. My hair had been like his once. I brushed the thought away, determined not to get into the poor-me mode today. I had plans.

After breakfast, I'd get dressed and maybe try to ride my bike into town. I wanted to find out if the sheriff had found out anything about the guy who'd run down Max. I also wanted to stop in at the realtor's office to see Charlie. I was pretty good at sizing people up, and I wanted to have a talk with the man Amelia called an old friend.

"Would you play a game with me?" Sam stepped back.

"Um. Maybe later, Sam. I have stuff to do." The microwave beeped. Mom took out the plate and set the steaming waffle and sizzling bacon in front of me.

"He's been waiting for you to get up, Jessie," Mom said. "He's missed you. Why don't you play with him for a while? His attention span isn't all that long."

Smiling down at Sam, I picked up the syrup and poured some on my waffle. "What do you want to play?"

"Monopoly." He tore off toward the family room where I could hear him opening the cupboard where we kept the games.

"He's terrible at that game."

Mom laughed. "Your dad's been helping him. You might be surprised."

I used my fork to slice a corner off the waffle. If Max didn't call by noon, I would call her.

Mom called me in a little before noon, but it wasn't to eat

lunch. Sam and I had gone from Monopoly to putting together a puzzle.

That's when they told me about Max being missing.

CHAPTER SIXTEEN

Like I said earlier, I tore up to my room and basically threw a fit. It took an hour for me to calm down. I knew I wasn't doing Max any good by crying. I needed to pull myself together and think this through.

I washed my face and got dressed in my jeans and a long-sleeved rust-colored top. Since the sun was out, I put on a floppy-brimmed denim hat with a pink and white peony-like flower holding the brim up in the front.

I found Mom in the laundry room folding clothes. "We have to do something."

She gave me a blank look. "Oh, you mean about Max. I don't see what that would be, Jessie. The police are looking for her."

"You said they think she ran away."

"That's a possibility."

"No. It isn't. Mom, she would never leave Amelia. Not with all this awful stuff going on. Somebody took her. I'll bet it was the same person who ran into her yesterday."

"Or maybe she got scared and ran away."

I started to argue and decided it wouldn't do me any good. I knew Mom wouldn't let me go anywhere alone, and I also knew she wouldn't take me where I needed to go. I went back up to my room and called Amelia.

"Mom told me about Max. Have you heard anything? Have the police found her?"

"Oh, Jessie, I don't know what to think. No. The police haven't found her. I know they have an Amber alert out, but I'm concerned they aren't taking her disappearance seriously."

"When did you last see her?" I asked.

"Last night. She helped me make up some sachets, and we both went to bed around 9:30. I gave her some pain pills, and I know she went to sleep because I checked on her around 11. Molly was barking about something, and I got up to make sure everything was locked."

"Molly was barking?"

"Yes, but I didn't see or hear anyone. I let her in and she settled right down. When I got up this morning at six, Max was gone. I've looked everywhere. There's no sign of her, but . . ."

"What?" I sensed doubt in her voice.

"She had gotten dressed. Her pajamas were lying on the bed, and her tennis shoes were gone. Her backpack was gone too. I suppose that's why the sheriff thought she had run away."

This wasn't looking good. I wondered if Max had gotten up during the night to go snooping around. I suggested this to Amelia.

"I suppose that's possible," she said. "We'd talked about the accident and went over everything that's happened. But where would she go? She didn't have her bike, and my boat is still in the boathouse."

I was getting more frustrated by the minute. I told Amelia I would be praying for Max and tried to sound hopeful. I had another idea I thought might work. Cooper Smally had been out of town, but maybe he was back by now. I dialed his number and dropped onto my bed.

"Hey, Cooper," I said when he answered. "Max is missing."

"What?" His voice sounded lower than I remembered, but then he was at that age. Puberty. I told him what had been happening while he'd been gone and explained what I wanted. "So can you come over? Mom won't let me go anywhere by myself, but if I'm with you . . ."

"Sure. I'll come. Are you sure you can ride your bike into town?"

"I think so. If I can't, I have an alternate plan."

"Okay. See you in about twenty minutes."

"Oh, wait. Do you have a camera?"

"Y-e-s." He drew out the word, apparently wanting an explanation.

"Bring it." I wasn't sure why, but every good detective needs a camera, and mine, thanks to a certain seagull, was at the bottom of the lake.

"Okay."

While I waited for Cooper, I went downstairs to look for Mom again and found her down by the dock watching Sam and the twins sail their boats in the shallow water. She had her easel set up and had started painting a background on a fresh canvas.

"Cooper is coming over," I said. "I was thinking about riding my bike into town."

She sighed. "I don't know if that's a good idea, Jessie." Worry lines made a V between her eyebrows.

"I'll be fine. If I get tired, I can call you to come get me."

Her gaze scanned my face, my clothes, and my feet. She was going to say no. "Dad would let me."

"I'm sure he would." The corners of her mouth turned up in a smile, but her eyes were still sad. "What would you do?"

"Just go into town. Maybe get chocolate-dipped strawberries at Cavanaugh's." I didn't tell her about my wanting to ask certain people questions.

"All right." She sighed again. "I suppose you can. I guess I'd be restless, too, if my best friend was missing."

"Yes!" I made a fist for emphasis.

She bit on her lower lip. "You and Cooper are going to look for Max, aren't you?"

I raised my head a little too fast. "I might. If she did run away, which I doubt, I know some places she might hide."

Mom nodded. "Just be careful. I want to talk to Cooper before you leave."

"Sure." I rolled my eyes as I turned back toward the house.

She'd give Cooper the same lecture she'd given Max about how fragile I was and how they needed to make sure I didn't overdo. But at least she'd said I could go. That was something.

I headed back inside. Up in my room I pulled a backpack out of my closet and stuffed in some things I might need. I had to bring my antibacterial hand cleaner, a face mask, and sunscreen. I put some of the sunscreen on my face and arms and dropped it into the bag. I also tucked in binoculars and a pad and pen, thinking I might need to take notes. I felt a little silly as I thought about what the girl detectives I'd read about would do in a case like this. Both Nancy Drew and Jennie McGrady would have had the case solved by now. But they weren't real, and they didn't have to worry about getting sick. I pushed the thoughts away. I wasn't a detective, but I had to figure out what was going on. Max's life, and maybe Amelia's, depended on it.

Cooper rang the doorbell just as my foot hit the last step on the stairs. I opened the door and took a step back. The guy standing on my doorstep couldn't have been Cooper Smally. Well, it was, but he had lost about forty pounds and grown at least two inches. "Um." I closed my mouth, embarrassed by the look I must have had on my face. "Wow," I managed to say. Cooper was actually pretty cute. "You look . . . different."

His red cheeks told me he was either sunburned or embarrassed. I suspected the latter. He looked down at me and crossed his arms. "You doing okay?"

"Yeah." I motioned for him to come in. "My mom wants to talk to you before we go."

"Look, I don't think you should ride your bike. You've only been out of the hospital for a couple of days, right?"

"How did you know?"

"I talked to Max last night."

"So you knew about the accident and everything?"

"Pretty much."

"You could have said something."

He shrugged, and when he didn't respond, I led him through the house and into the backyard.

"Hi, Mrs. Miller," he said.

Mom did a double take when she saw him, but didn't comment. "Hi, Cooper. How was your trip to Oregon?"

"Good." He nodded.

"Jessie tells me you two are going to look for Max. That's fine, but please keep in mind that she has a tendency to do too much."

"Don't worry, Mrs. Miller. I brought a bike buggy for Jessie to ride in. I figured she'd never make it into town on her own."

Mom smiled. "Good thinking." She tossed me a look that said she thought I was in good hands.

A few minutes later, I started across the lawn, trying not to feel annoyed. One of these days I'd be able to go somewhere and do something without my family and friends thinking I was breakable. "Come on. We need to get going."

I climbed into the buggy, glad it had a cover so no one could see me. If I'd been much bigger, I wouldn't have fit into it, but it was actually pretty comfortable, and after a while I was glad to have the ride. I even unzipped the cover so I could see better.

When we got into town, Cooper stopped in front of the tea shop. Ivy was working, so I told her the news about Max, but she'd already heard. "The police were here asking about her." She rested her arms on the top of the counter, her eyes swooping over to Cooper and then back to me. "Do you think she ran away?"

"Not unless someone was after her." My gaze roamed down to the chocolate-dipped strawberries. I asked for four. After paying for them, I offered two to Cooper. "We decided to look for Max just in case," I said to Ivy.

"Thanks," Cooper said. "I'll be outside when you're ready." He popped one of the strawberries into his mouth and once outside tossed the stem into a trash can.

"What's with him?" Ivy asked, her admiring gaze still following him.

I shrugged. "I have no idea."

"He sure has changed."

"I hadn't noticed," I teased as I ate one of the juicy berries. They were extra good this time of year, probably because the berries were grown just outside of town.

I frowned. "Do you know anything about Max? Did the police say anything when they came in?" A lot of people came into the Tea and Candy Shoppe since it was one of the best places around for lunch, desserts, coffee, and tea. Right now there were three women in the farthest corner, wearing red hats with purple feathers and laughing.

"One thing. I don't know if it will help. They found the truck that hit her yesterday. It was parked in the lot at Hansons grocery store in Lakeside. It had been stolen from one of the migrant worker families. They'd reported it missing yesterday."

"None of this makes sense. If you hear anything let me know."

"I will." She lowered her voice as a man came into the shop. "I have to get back to work. Let *me* know if *you* hear anything."

I turned around and nearly bumped into a heavyset man with silver hair. He took hold of my shoulder with his left hand to steady me. "Whoa there." He chuckled. "You're Jessie Miller, aren't you?"

"Yeah."

He let me go. "Charlie O'Donnell. O'Donnell Realty. I know your folks."

"Oh, right." I smiled back. "You're a friend of Mrs. Truesdale's, aren't you?"

Cooper came in and stood behind Charlie, wanting to know what I wanted to do. Since Charlie had been on my list of people to talk to, I decided this might be a good time. "I can't believe how lucky we are," I said. "Cooper and I would like to ask you about Amelia."

His expression changed to one of concern. "Hmm. Yes. Nasty business, that. I was just going to have my afternoon coffee. Why don't you join me?"

Cooper and I followed him to a table by the window and sat across from him.

I wanted to come right out and ask him what he'd done with Max. Instead, I asked if he knew that Max was missing.

"I think everyone in town knows about the girl." He folded his paper and rested his thick arms on the table.

I could tell from his build that he wasn't the man Max and I had seen leave Amelia's house that night. Of course, that didn't mean he couldn't have hired someone. "Do you know of anyone who might want Amelia's land enough to force her to leave? I mean, when you look at all that's happened, her tire slashed, her house broken into, her roadside stand vandalized, and then Max getting hit . . . it seems like someone wants to force Amelia to leave her farm."

He pushed his cheek out with his tongue. "I know a lot of people who wouldn't mind having that property, but not one of them would ever think about causing her harm."

"How can you be sure?"

He smiled. "The sheriff just asked me the same thing. I gave him a list of the people I know of who've shown an interest in Amelia's land for the last year. I imagine they'll sort through it. It might be a good idea if you just let them take care of it."

I didn't think I'd get anything else out of him, but I did have one more question. "How much is the land worth?"

He rubbed his chin, and for a second, I didn't think he'd answer me. "Well, that depends. There was a developer from

California a while back who was willing to pay $15 million. I took his offer to Amelia, but she turned it down flat."

Cooper whistled. "That's a lot of money."

"You bet it is." Charlie clucked his tongue and shook his head. "Personally, I think the woman is crazy. Deals like that don't come along every day, and sooner or later she's going to have to sell. She's no spring chicken, you know."

"Huh?" Cooper frowned.

"It means she's old," I said.

"Oh."

Charlie leaned back when Ivy brought his coffee and a scone. He lifted his cup and inhaled. I couldn't see what was so special about coffee. Mom tells me I'll change my mind someday, but I doubt it. "This guy from California, where is he now?"

The corners of Charlie's mouth turned down. "I have no idea."

"What did he look like?" I asked.

"Light brown hair, about five ten, brown eyes. Nice-looking fellow."

That described half the men in town, including my father. "Has Max talked to you in the last day or two?"

He pursed his lips, took a sip, and let out a sigh. "I haven't seen your friend. Like I said, I hope the police are able to locate her. Now if you don't mind . . ."

I nodded. "Come on, Coop, let's go see if the sheriff has learned anything." I turned back and thanked Charlie even though he hadn't given me all that much information.

We got even less information from the sheriff. He hadn't found Max, and he told Cooper and me that we should mind our own business. He reminded me about the last time I'd tried to play detective. "You might not be so lucky next time."

I don't like being reminded of my foolish choices. And he seemed to forget that if it hadn't been for me, the cops might not have caught those drug dealers.

When we got back to Cooper's bike, he suggested we ride up to the waterfalls.

"That's a good idea." I'd found Max there once after her uncle had used her for a punching bag. "If she did run away, she might be hiding from somebody, and there are a lot of places to hide in the park."

"There are a lot of places to hide around here, period. Max could be anywhere." There was something in his tone that told me he was as worried as I was.

We didn't find her at the park or see any sign of her in the places where she liked to hang out.

"I should take you back home, Jessie." Cooper tipped his head to one side and gave me an I'm-worried-about-you look.

"We can't give up. Besides, we haven't looked everywhere."

CHAPTER SEVENTEEN

I closed my eyes and rested the whole way back to my house. I had talked Cooper into rowing the boat over to Amelia's place. I really needed to find out what the guy took from the attic, and I wanted a chance to look around for Max.

"I want to see how Amelia is doing," I told Mom once we got to my house. "She's probably really worried, and I bet she could use the company."

"That's a nice gesture." Mom hugged me. "I may try to go over later. Tell her we're praying."

"I will." I fed Cooper and me tuna sandwiches, some carrot sticks, and an apple. When we'd eaten, I grabbed a couple of bottles of water, some crackers, and cheese sticks and stuffed them in my backpack. I wasn't sure how long the trip would take because I planned on searching the farm for Max or for clues that might tell us where she was.

We put on life jackets and climbed into the boat. The lake was calm and the surface smooth. Cooper rowed and I trailed my hand in the water. One thing hadn't changed about Cooper. He still didn't say a lot, which was okay with me.

After a while my curiosity got the best of me. "How did you lose so much weight, Cooper? I mean, you've changed so much, I almost didn't recognize you."

He snorted. "My dad and I went to a camp for fat people. He said it was time for both of us to start eating healthy and lose weight."

I smiled. "It worked. Did he lose weight too?"

"Yeah." Cooper didn't seem to want to talk about it, so I dropped the subject.

After a while, Cooper rested the oars on his knees and took a drink of the bottled water. "Max said the bone marrow transplant was supposed to keep you from getting sick again."

The sun was shining in my eyes, and I looked at him through narrow slits. "We're hoping," I said.

He nodded. "You look better. Not so pale."

I laughed. "Probably because I've been in the sun a lot the last few days."

He picked up the oars and started rowing again. Several minutes later he asked, "Why do you think Max decided to move in with Mrs. Truesdale?"

"I'm not sure. Max told me she thought Amelia could use someone to help her out. Maybe Max wants a family of her own."

"Hard to think of Mrs. Truesdale and Max as a family. A family is a mom and dad and kids. Like yours."

"Hmm. I guess I never really thought about that. You and your dad are a family."

"Not anymore."

"Sure you are. Just because your mom died doesn't mean you stop being a family." Seeing the hurt look on Cooper's face, I wished I could have taken the words back. "I'm sorry."

"For what?" Cooper turned away from me and stared at the shoreline. He didn't speak again until we rowed up to Amelia's dock.

Amelia must have seen us coming because she was heading toward us waving. Molly trotted ahead, barking and wagging her tail. "Jessie, your mother called to tell me you and Cooper were coming. I'm glad you're here." She helped Cooper tie the boat up and waited for us to climb out onto the dock. "I've been baking most of the day. Are you interested in some blackberry shortcake?"

"Sure," Cooper said.

"I just ate, but I'd like some tea." Being on the lake had given me chills. I ended up eating a small piece of scone though, which she'd topped with whipped cream.

Once we'd eaten, I asked Amelia if she had ever gone up in the attic to look around. "Maybe if you knew what that guy took, you'd know who did all the other stuff." *And who took Max.* I didn't say the last part out loud. I worried that the guy who had run her off the road had come back to finish the job. *Please, God, let Max be safe.*

"I haven't had a chance." Amelia took the dishes to the sink and washed the crumbs off the table. "But it's a good idea. Why don't the two of you come up with me?"

I followed them up to the second floor without much trouble, but halfway up to the attic, my knees gave out. Cooper came back and took me piggyback the rest of the way. When we got to the top, he straightened and I slid off his back. "Thanks," I said. "Sorry to be so much trouble." I adjusted my denim hat.

"You're light." Cooper looked me over. "Are you sure you want to do this? Your mom said you were supposed to take it easy."

"I'm fine." I sounded snippy, but did everyone think they had to feel responsible for me?

"Okay." He lifted his hands in surrender. "Forget I asked."

Sunlight filtered in through four dirty windows. Amelia made her way to the center of the room and pulled a cord, switching on the bare lightbulb. A thick layer of dust covered everything. The first thing I noticed was the two sets of footprints leading to an old trunk. I pointed them out to Amelia. "Did the deputy walk around in here?"

"No. He just stood on the stairs and shined the flashlight around. I doubt he could even see them from where he was standing."

The larger set of prints probably belonged to the man who'd been in the attic our first night there. The second set was much smaller, and I guessed they belonged to Max. Which meant she'd been up here without Amelia. Maybe Max had been doing some detective work on her own. Maybe she found something she shouldn't have. I pointed the footprints out to Amelia.

"It's possible Max came up here," Amelia said. "I don't really mind, but I wish she'd have said something."

"She might have been looking for clues." I followed Amelia and Cooper to the trunk.

Amelia knelt down in front of it. "I'm not sure I could tell if anything is missing. I don't even remember what all was in here. This was my father's. I did go through some of his things years and years ago." She frowned and moved some papers around. "Something *is* missing, Jessie. The map and a journal. It's a surveyor's map, and it was rolled up in a canister."

"Why would anyone take a map?" Cooper asked.

"This wasn't just any map. My grandfather found gold here back in the 1800s, or so the story goes. As I recall, he mined for several years, but he put more money into mining than he made by selling the gold. Eventually, the vein ran out, and he went back to farming. I haven't thought about that mine in years."

"Does your son know about it?" I asked.

She nodded. "My father used to tell him stories, but Freddy wouldn't have broken in here to steal the map. As I said before, all he had to do was ask."

"So, the map tells where the mine is—sort of like a treasure map?" Cooper rocked back on his heels.

"I suppose so." Amelia sorted through the other paraphernalia in the trunk before closing it and letting Cooper help her up.

"Does Charlie know about the map or the mine?" I asked.

"I don't know." Amelia dusted off her jeans. "I suppose some of the old-timers around here might know. My grandfather hired a few men to work the mine. Like I said, he closed it down after a while because there was no profit in it."

I had an idea. "Whoever took the map must have been interested in finding the mine. Charlie told us there was a developer from California who offered $15 million. Maybe he thinks there's still gold in it. Maybe he read about it, or Charlie told him."

"How would he know to look in the attic?" Cooper asked.

"Logic?" I felt my excitement growing. "Maybe this isn't the first time he's been here."

"Do you know where the mine is?" Cooper asked Amelia.

"I used to." Amelia headed for the stairwell. "I might be able to find it. It's in the foothills. There's an old road that would take us there, but it's probably overgrown. I haven't been out there in years."

"I think we should go," I said. "Max could have found out about it. We should see if anybody's been there."

"You think Max might be in the mine?" Cooper waited for us at the stairs.

"It's possible." I let Cooper give me a piggyback ride down the stairs. If we were going to look for that mine, I wanted to save my strength.

CHAPTER EIGHTEEN

Amelia took her keys off the hook by the door and went outside. "I wonder if I should call the sheriff to let him know where we're going in case something happens."

"I have my cell phone," I said, not wanting to waste any more time.

"All right, then. We'll need flashlights and jackets. Jessie, they're in the closet in the entry. I'll grab some snacks in case we're out there longer than we expect. I have an emergency kit in the pickup. A couple of those silver blankets, matches, things like that."

"We're only going to be out there for a couple of hours, aren't we?" Cooper dug his hands into his pockets.

"Hopefully we'll be back before supper," Amelia told him. "But my father taught me to always be prepared for anything. Living here in the mountains, you can bet I take that advice literally."

We got into the front seat of the pickup, with me in the middle. Instead of driving down the driveway, Amelia took us around the barn, through the pasture, and between two big lavender fields. The lavender fields ended at a large outcropping of rocks. I thought the road had ended too, but Amelia maneuvered over rocky ground and then behind the hill. The road wound around several rock-faced cliffs. Except for two narrow tracks for tires, shrubs and grass covered the flat areas.

"You might be right, Jessie," Amelia said. "Someone has been out here. See the berry vines? Someone has trimmed them back."

I looked to where she pointed, and my stomach lurched. Maybe coming out here wasn't the best idea. Suppose the guy was here? Branches scraped the side of the truck on both sides. We'd have a hard time turning around if we needed to make a quick get-away. I took a deep breath. *We'll be okay,* I told myself. I had the cell so we could call for help.

We came into a small clearing and Amelia stopped, turned around, and aimed the pickup back the way we'd come. "I think the mine opening is just beyond this outcropping of rocks."

"Wow. I can't believe you have a real mine on your property." Cooper held the door open while I climbed out.

"I know it sounds exciting, but I hope I can trust the two of you not to come out here snooping around, and please don't tell anyone. Mines can be dangerous, and this one is no exception. My brother fell down a steep hole near the back of this one and broke his leg. It was the last time any of us was allowed to come here. My father boarded it up and posted a no-trespassing sign." Amelia pulled a pack out of the back of the truck and slung it over her arm. She handed each of us a flashlight. "We'll go in and have a look around, but only in the first chamber. It has a rock surface—

like a cave. In the tunnels the wood beams are undoubtedly rotten, so no exploring there."

We both agreed and followed her over and around the rocks. If her grandfather had meant to hide the mine, he'd done a good job. The entry was a natural-looking cave with a small offset entrance we couldn't see until we were a few feet away.

"Obviously someone has been here." The barricade she'd mentioned earlier had been dismantled. Amelia ducked in first, telling us to wait while she made sure it was safe. A few minutes later, she told us to come in. "Just watch out for the bats."

I motioned for Cooper to go first while I worked up the courage to step inside. Bats were not my favorite species. The entrance to the mine smelled musty and damp. I clicked on my flashlight and waved it around. One of the bats hanging from the ceiling opened its yellow eyes and closed them again. I hoped it stayed put.

"The actual mine shaft is over here." Amelia held her flashlight high and illuminated about a four-by-six opening. Again she told us to wait while she went inside. She came out minutes later looking pale and shaken.

"Someone has been here recently, but I didn't see any sign of Max."

"Could she be back inside somewhere?"

"I hope not." She bit her bottom lip. "It's time to call the sheriff."

"Okay. My cell phone is in the pickup in my backpack. I'll go get it."

I hurried back to the truck and climbed inside. I'd put my

pack behind the seat and had to practically lie down to get at it. I was just about to dial when I heard a car engine. I backed out of the cab and eased the door shut. Not wanting to be caught in the open until I knew who it was, I ran to an outcropping of brush and crouched down behind it. An older-model dark green truck came into view. The driver was a man—middle-aged, I guessed, brown hair and unshaven. He wore jeans and a long-sleeved cowboy shirt and hat. I'd seen him before, probably in town. I swallowed hard, thinking this could be the guy Max and I had seen getting into the boat that night.

A deep frown etched his tanned face as he stared at Amelia's truck and looked around. When he headed for the cave, my heart slammed into overdrive. I wanted to warn Amelia and Cooper, but warning them would alert the cowboy to my presence too, and I decided I'd be better off hiding until I knew for sure what was going on. When I felt like he was out of earshot, I pulled out my cell phone and started to dial 911. I could barely hear the dispatch operator, and after several attempts to tell her I needed the sheriff, I realized she couldn't hear me at all. I tried again, but the phone was dead. *The batteries.* How long had it been since someone had recharged the phone?

Not knowing what else to do, I kept under cover and moved closer to the cave.

"Mrs. Truesdale?" I heard the cowboy yell. Maybe she and Cooper had heard the truck coming like me, and had taken cover. But he knew Amelia was here because of the pickup.

"Martin, is that you?" Amelia called back.

I let myself breathe and relax a little. Martin was the man Amelia had hired to replace Carlos.

"What are you doing clear out here?" he asked.

"I could ask you the same thing."

I moved forward and plastered myself against a rock wall not far from the cave's entrance, where I could see, but duck out of sight if I had to.

"Actually, I was looking for you," Martin said. "When I turned in the driveway, I thought I saw the pickup, so I followed you out here. I just got back into town this morning. I imagine you got a pretty long list of things for me to do."

"As a matter of fact, I do. First things first though." Amelia stepped out of the cave and walked several steps to meet Martin. Cooper wasn't with her. She glanced around, and I had a feeling she was looking for me.

Martin took off his hat and ran a hand through his hair. "What are you doing here at the mine?"

"You know about the mine?"

He shrugged. "Sure. I ran into it soon after I started working here."

"You were hired to work in the lavender fields, not explore caves."

He smiled. "Sorry about that, ma'am. I saw the road, and it looked like someone had been out here recently. I wanted to know where the tracks led. Didn't take me long to find the cave. I realized it was a mine. I checked the records for any mining done in the area, and sure enough. Saw that your grandfather had mined it for several years. I was going to ask you about it before I had that family emergency."

She smiled back at him, apparently believing his story. I wasn't that trusting.

"Quite a lot has happened since you left, Martin." She told him about the guy breaking into the house and the vandalism.

"I'm sorry I wasn't here. Did the cops catch him?"

"No, but that's not the half of it." She told him about Max coming to live with her and the accident. They kept walking and soon reached his truck. I followed as best I could. So far Amelia hadn't said anything about Cooper or me, and I wasn't sure why. Maybe she didn't trust him completely either. And speaking of Cooper . . . I glanced back at the cave but didn't see any sign of him.

For a minute, I thought Amelia was going to follow Martin back to the farm and leave Cooper and me stranded. She asked Martin to call the sheriff and have him or one of his deputies come out. He pulled a cell phone off the holder on his belt and handed the phone to her.

"Thanks." She dialed 911 and told the operator she needed the sheriff to come out right away and to bring the medical examiner.

Medical examiner? I sank onto the ground, my knees no longer able to support me. Calling in an ME meant only one thing. She'd found a body. But why hadn't she said anything to Cooper and me? *It's not Max,* I told myself over and over. *It can't be. It just can't.*

CHAPTER NINETEEN

While Amelia and Martin were talking, I went back to the cave to find Cooper. "Cooper?" I whispered in as loud a voice as I dared.

He stepped out of one of the crevices. "Shh." He pulled me back into his hiding place and kept his hand on my shoulder.

"What's going on?" I whispered.

"I don't know. We heard a truck come up, and Mrs. T said I should stay out of sight. When the guy called her name, she told me to stay where I was while she went out to talk to him. Where were you?"

"He drove up when I went to get the cell phone. All I could think to do was hide. Amelia called the sheriff and said he should bring the medical examiner. Why would she do that unless . . . ?"

Cooper hesitated. "Mrs. T found a body back there—in the mine."

"Not Max." My stomach hurt. Tears pricked my eyes.

Cooper shook his head. "I don't know who it is. That Martin guy showed up before she could tell me."

I covered my face with my hands and squeezed my eyes shut.

This wasn't happening. In a minute or two I would wake up and Max would be safe. I hugged myself and leaned against the rock wall.

"Jessie?" Amelia called my name twice, and then she and Martin stepped back into the cave. "The body is decomposed," Amelia said to Martin, "but from the clothes, I'm thinking it might be Carlos." She glanced around. "Cooper? Jessie? Are you in here?"

Cooper stepped out into the open. "We're right here."

"Oh, Jessie," Amelia grabbed me as I staggered to my feet and pulled me into a hug. "I was so worried. Where did you go?"

"I heard Martin's truck and thought I'd better hide. My cell phone was dead, so I couldn't call the sheriff."

"It's okay. I used Martin's phone to call him."

"I know." I was shaking and couldn't seem to get my legs to work.

"Martin, would you carry Jessie out to the truck? In fact, why don't you take her and Cooper back to the house? That way you can meet the sheriff and bring him out with you."

"Sure thing."

I did not want to go anywhere with Martin. Amelia seemed to trust him, but I didn't. As it turned out, I didn't have anything to worry about. He didn't say much while he drove us back to the house. Martin carried me inside and set me down gently on the couch in the living room, and then he went outside. I'd almost decided I could trust him. Cooper and I watched him from the living room window. The sheriff came in about the same time with a van following—probably the medical examiner. They talked for a minute, and then Martin hopped into the sheriff's Blazer and they drove off toward the hills.

I fluffed up the pillows on the couch and stretched out. Cooper kept staring out the window. "I don't like it," he said. "Carlos has been missing for over a month, and now they find him in the mine shaft."

"I know." I swallowed hard, tears stinging my eyes again. "And now Max is missing."

Cooper glanced at his watch. "I need to call my dad and tell him what's going on."

I nodded, closing my eyes when he left the room. I could hear him telling his dad where he was. I took off my hat and felt it drop to the floor.

It was dark when I woke up. Amelia was sitting in the rocker with her feet up, and Mom was in the overstuffed chair. Sam sat on the rug petting Molly.

"Hey." Mom came over to the couch and ran her hand over my head.

"What are you doing here? Where's Cooper and . . . Max?"

Mom's head moved from side to side. "She's still missing, Jessie. Cooper's dad came out to get him."

She helped me sit up. "You've had a rough day. Amelia's been telling me."

"The body you found . . ." I rubbed my eyes. "Was it Carlos?"

"I'm afraid so," Amelia said. "His wallet was still on him."

Mom waited for me to sit up, then wrapped an arm around my shoulders. "Are you ready to go home?"

"Not really," I said. "Couldn't I stay here? I want to be here if they find Max, and I don't want Amelia to be alone."

Mom pinched her lips together and looked over at Amelia.

"I'd be happy for the company." Amelia smiled at me. "If you think she'll be okay."

"I'll be fine, Mom. I was just tired. I don't have a fever or anything."

"All right. I'll go home and pack some things for you."

I hugged her. "Thanks."

While my mother went to get my overnight bag, Amelia fed me dinner. "Nothing fancy," she said, "just tomato soup and grilled cheese sandwiches."

"That's okay." I didn't feel much like eating anyway. "Mrs. Truesdale, I'm sorry about Carlos. He was nice."

"Yes, he was." She reached into her pocket and pulled out a tissue and used it to wipe her eyes. "I never did believe he'd gone back to Mexico. I'm more worried about Max than ever. Carlos was murdered. The medical examiner said he'd been stabbed. If there are defense wounds, they're hoping to get DNA that will lead them to the killer."

I'd watched a few crime shows and knew mostly what she was talking about.

I also knew that with real cops, finding criminals wasn't that easy. "So you're sure Max wasn't in the cave?"

"Not that anyone could see. The sheriff had his deputies go through the tunnels." She placed cheese between slices of bread and buttered the top of each sandwich. The buttered bread sizzled when she set the sandwiches into the heated frying pan. I rested my head on my arms thinking I should help set the table or something, but I couldn't seem to move out of the chair. Max had been missing for eighteen hours, but it felt like days. I wasn't sure I wanted to stay with Amelia now. I felt restless and sick to my stomach. All I wanted to do was find Max, but I wasn't sure what I could do. She could be anywhere. If the cops couldn't find her, what made me think I could? Maybe if I could figure out who had killed Carlos . . .

"What do you know about Martin?" I asked. "He's not from around here, is he?"

"He's from the Seattle area—has family there. He's new to Chenoa Lake. There's no reason to suspect him of killing Carlos. Carlos was gone before Martin moved here. He had only worked for me for a couple of weeks when his father had a heart attack. Most of the past two weeks he's been in Seattle."

I nodded, trying to remember why he looked familiar to me. If what Amelia said was true, then I couldn't have seen him before I went into the hospital. Which meant I must have seen him after I got out—within the last few days. Of course, he could just look like someone I know.

While we were eating, Mom came back with my bag. Amelia asked her to sit and eat with us, but Mom said she had to get back.

"Your father got the contract to design the mansion for Mr. Porter, and he's taking me out to celebrate."

"Cool," I said, remembering the rich John Porter and his black Cadillac.

When Mom left, I helped Amelia with the dishes. After that we worked on lavender sachets for a while, but it wasn't the same without Max.

"Max will be okay," I told her. "She's tough."

"I hope so. If I'd had any idea that being associated with me would bring her harm, I wouldn't have asked her to stay. She was far better off at your house."

"It isn't your fault," I insisted.

"I know, but I can't help but wonder. Maybe if I had done as Freddy asked and moved into town, none of this would have happened."

I wasn't sure what to say. I still thought Freddy might be involved, but didn't think this was the time to say so. At nine, Amelia locked the doors and we walked up the stairs together. I counted the creaks—five in all—and the last one was in front of Max's room. Amelia didn't seem to notice them. I might not have either if not for the burglar from the other night. "Good night," I said when I went into Max's room.

"Good night, Jessie. I think we should pray extra hard tonight that the police find Max and that she's all right."

"I will."

I dropped onto the extra bed and sat staring across the room where Max had slept. I don't know why—maybe I just needed to feel closer to her—but I crossed the room and curled up on her bed. "Where are you, Max?" I closed my eyes tight and tried to make my mind hook up with hers. I'd read about twins who could read each other's minds. Max and I were close, and sometimes I knew what she was thinking, but as hard as I tried to connect with her, nothing happened.

I eyed the bag Mom had brought, thinking I should get up and put on my pajamas, but I didn't move. Instead I lay there thinking about all the things that had happened. I felt almost certain that the driver who tried to run down Max was the same person who had killed Carlos. I thought about Fred again, but how could he hurt his own mother like that? Besides, he didn't need to break into the house to get the map. I'd ruled Charlie out because of his size. He was much fatter than the man Max and I had seen getting into the boat that first night we'd stayed here. That left Martin or someone we hadn't met yet.

I must have dozed off, because I woke up with a jolt around midnight. I'd heard something. There it was again—a creak on the stairs. I threw the covers aside and headed for the closet.

It's probably Amelia.

Or not.

The doorknob turned. A chill shuddered through me. I grabbed the knitted throw from the back of the chair and pulled it around me as I moved into the closet and quietly pulled the door closed. Every sound seemed magnified, though I doubted Amelia could hear a thing. The door opened and someone stepped inside. I curled up tighter and stopped breathing. All I could hope for now was that the intruder couldn't see or hear me. I peeked through the slit in the closet door and ducked back when an elongated shadow filled the doorway. Something the sheriff said to Amelia pounded in my ears. "If they wanted the land, why not just kill you?"

He's back, and this time he's going to kill Amelia.

CHAPTER TWENTY

I flattened out against the wall wishing I could make myself invisible.

If he was going to kill Amelia, why would he come into Max's room? Of course, he might not know which room was hers, but something didn't seem right. And if he did plan to kill Amelia, why was he still here? With the door partly open, I leaned forward for a better look.

My breath came rushing out when I saw who it was. I pushed the closet door open farther and stood in the doorway with my arms folded. "Where have you been?"

The girl I thought was my best friend whirled around and glared at me. "Jess, you nearly scared me to death. What are you doing here?"

"I have been looking everywhere for you." This wasn't at all the reunion I expected to have if I ever saw Max again. She seemed furious with me, and to be honest, I wasn't too happy with her either. "Everyone has," I said. "I thought you'd been kidnapped. I told them you wouldn't run away. I told them you hadn't stolen anything, but you did run away, didn't you? And what about Amelia's missing money? Did you take that too?"

Max looked at me for a minute, then pulled me the rest of the way out of the closet. "We have to talk."

"I'm not sure I have anything to say to you." My eyes filled up, and I brushed them away with my sleeve.

"Look, this wasn't my idea. I had no choice. I had to leave."

I dropped onto the bed. "What are you talking about?"

"This guy told me if I didn't leave town for good, he'd kill me."

"Seriously?" Feeling suddenly cold, I wrapped the throw tighter around myself.

"I wouldn't lie to you, Jess."

"Then why are you here?"

"I came back to get some things."

I closed my eyes trying to understand. "You can't just leave again."

"I have to. Don't you see? I don't have any proof that this guy did anything."

"You know who he is?"

"No . . . I . . ." She bit into her lower lip. "He must have taken the money from Mrs. T and framed me. I can't turn myself in. No one will believe me."

She was probably right about that. As much as I wanted to, I wasn't sure I believed her myself. "Start from the beginning. Tell me everything."

Max glanced at the door, looking like she was about to bolt.

Instead she moved to the window and lifted a slat in the blinds to look outside. "Okay. The night after the hit-and-run, Mrs. T and I went to bed early, but I woke up around 11 and couldn't sleep. I went downstairs. I was reading when the phone rang. This guy told me I had to do exactly what he said or he'd kill me. He told me there was a boat waiting for me at the dock and an envelope with a thousand dollars cash in it plus a bus ticket to Portland."

"Oh, Max."

"He said if I tried to contact anybody, he'd kill me and you."

"Me?"

"I think that was just to scare me into doing what he wanted for sure." She came back and sat on her bed. "I know this sounds crazy, but he gave me a thousand dollars cash and a bus ticket to Portland. All I had to do was promise to leave for good."

"But you didn't go to Portland or leave for good."

"No." She sighed. "I couldn't. I rowed up to Lakeside, and when the stores opened, I bought some camping supplies and went out to the island to lay low for a while."

I pressed my hands against my eyes. I wanted to believe her, but I sensed that Max wasn't being totally honest with me. "You know who it is, don't you?"

She shook her head. "I can't tell you that. Anyway, I'm not positive. I have to go."

"What did you come back for?"

"This." She held up her journal. "And I wanted to give Mrs. T back the money he took from her."

I walked out into the hallway with her and down the steps. "I should scream right now and wake up Mrs. T. Then you'll have to stay."

"No!" Max stopped and I ran into her, nearly knocking us both down the stairs. "Didn't you hear what I said? If we tell the sheriff any of this, the guy will kill us."

"What if he's bluffing?"

She turned around and started back down the stairs. "What if he isn't? We can't risk it."

I didn't know what to do. I couldn't keep Max there, but . . . "Maybe I should go with you."

With a heavy sigh she turned around again and grabbed my shoulders. "You can't."

"Carlos is dead," I said. "He was murdered."

"What?"

I told her about the mine and how Amelia had found his body. "You can't leave, Max. You need to help me find out who killed him and who wants you out of the way. If you know anything . . ."

Max let go of me, looking even more worried than before. "He's not bluffing. Carlos knew too much, and it got him killed. Do you want that to happen to us too?"

"At least tell me where you're going."

She shook her head and let herself out. I stood in the shadows, watching her jog down to the dock and get into the boat. I stood there for a long time. No way could I sleep now. I had to figure out how to help Max. Pulling the throw tighter around myself, I went downstairs to the living room. *God, please keep her safe. Should I wake up Amelia and tell her Max was here? Maybe I'll tell her in the morning.*

It was at that moment I realized I was not alone. The downstairs was dark except for the light coming in through the windows from the yard light. Still, I could see the menacing form of a man standing in the entry. I couldn't see his face, but I doubted it would do me any good if I could identify him. Unless I could outrun him, I'd never see another sunrise.

CHAPTER
TWENTY-ONE

I screamed and bolted for the front door. The throw dropped to the floor. I screamed again, hoping it was loud enough to wake Amelia. Once outside, I ran into the barn through the big doors, but instead of looking for a place to hide, I went out through the small side door and waited. The man's footsteps pounded across the gravel and into the barn. *Please let him think I'm hiding in there.* I heard him thrashing around the barn, his flashlight swinging back and forth.

While he tore through the barn, I crept back to the house and slipped inside, then closed and locked the door.

"Jessie?"

"Yikes!" I spun around.

Amelia stood in the middle of the living room in her pajamas. "What's going on? I heard screaming." She pulled me into a hug when I stepped closer.

"He's out there." I could barely squeeze the words through my throat. "The one who . . ." I hesitated when I saw Molly standing beside Amelia. Molly hadn't barked when the guy came in, which meant only one thing. Molly knew the intruder. "He's looking for me in the barn, but it won't take him very long to realize I'm not in there, and then he'll come back inside."

"Wait right here." All traces of sleep had left Amelia's eyes as she ducked into the closet by the door. When she backed out, she had a rifle. "You stay out of sight. I'll have a little surprise for our guest when he comes back."

I placed a hand on her arm. "You can't shoot him. It's Fred."

"Are you sure?" She looked suddenly pale and older.

"I think so. Molly didn't bark."

We both looked up when someone stuck a key in the lock. The door opened, and Fred Truesdale stepped inside. Surprise registered on his face when he saw his mother holding the gun. "What . . . ? Mother, put that thing away before you hurt someone."

Amelia lowered the shotgun. "I think you have some explaining to do. For starters you might want to tell me what you're doing here in the middle of the night."

"I drove in from Portland after work and thought I'd just crash here. I came in and saw her." He nodded toward me. "When she screamed and ran, I naturally thought she was up to no good, so I went after her."

"I thought you were going to kill me." My reaction seemed silly now, but at the time I didn't realize it was him.

"I'm sorry if I frightened you, Jessie. That wasn't my intention."

"Well, Fred," Amelia said, "maybe you should call next time

you decide to come in this late. What did you want to see me about?" Amelia asked.

"I've been thinking a lot about the farm and you and this business about you wanting a foster kid. I was wrong to try to push you into retiring. I came out to tell you I'm sorry and I won't stand in your way. When I saw how determined you've been through all this . . ." He waved his arm. "The vandalism and getting your tires slashed, and the business with Max and Carlos."

I didn't believe him. "So you're saying you didn't do any of those things?"

"Of course not. I love my mother and wouldn't do anything to harm her."

"What about Max?" I asked.

Fred thrummed his fingers on the table. He looked at his mother. "I still think getting a foster child at your age is nuts, but . . ."

"What about me?" The familiar voice came from the front room.

I jumped up, knocking over the chair in the process. "Max!" I threw my arms around her when she came into the kitchen. "You came back."

"So the sheriff was right," Amelia said. "You did run away."

"Not exactly. I bought some camping gear and stayed on an island not far from here. I decided it just wasn't right. I never should have left. I'm sorry, Mrs. T."

Amelia nodded. "I'm glad you're back."

"I didn't steal your money, Mrs. T." Max told them about being threatened and forced to leave town.

Fred pinched the bridge of his nose. "That's quite a story, Miss Hunter. But I don't believe a word of it."

She looked over at me. "I told you they wouldn't believe me."

"On the contrary, Max," Amelia said. "I believe you. Can you identify the man's voice?"

"I'm not sure. I think he disguised it."

"I have an idea," I said. "Where's the money, Max?"

"I brought it back earlier and set it in Mrs. T's sewing room."

I asked Max to get it. "What are you thinking, Jess?" she asked.

"We should have the sheriff check the envelope and the money for fingerprints. Whoever took the money is probably the one who did all the other stuff too."

"Good thinking, Jessie," Amelia said.

"There's no need for that." Fred sighed, then leaned forward and lowered his head to his hands. "I took the money and sent Max away. I should have known she wouldn't do as she was told."

Amelia stared at him like he'd turned into Dracula. "How could you?"

Fred got up and walked to the sink as if he needed to put some distance between himself and his mother. He turned around and leaned back against the counter. "I was desperate for you to sell this place, Mother. I wanted to wear you down. I knew if Max stayed, you'd dig your heels in even more than you had before. I realize now it was a mistake."

"I'm confused," I said. "Why would you run Max off the road, and then later pay her to leave town?"

"I didn't do any of those things except take money and try to pay off Max." He glanced at his mother. "I wanted it to look like Max had taken the money and run away so you would rethink your decision."

"There's more to it than that," Amelia said. "Why were you so intent on my selling the farm?"

"Things haven't been going so good for my business, and the farm is losing money. You kept turning down offers on the house. I was getting desperate."

"I should have you arrested." Amelia checked her watch. "But I won't. At least not tonight. I think we should all go to bed and finish talking about this in the morning."

After giving Fred some bedding for the sofa, Amelia came upstairs with Max and me. "I'm glad you're back, Max. I'm so sorry Fred put you through this."

"Sorry about spending some of the money," Max said. "I'll find a way to pay you back."

Amelia hugged her. "You'll do no such thing. Now, off to bed with you both. I have a feeling we'll all be sleeping in this morning."

Max fell asleep right away, but it took me a while. I kept thinking about Fred's money problems. He'd confessed to threatening Max and taking the money, but I felt like he wasn't telling us everything. And I had this nagging feeling things were going to get worse. Much worse.

CHAPTER
TWENTY-TWO

It didn't take long for me to realize my intuition had been right on.

I was almost asleep when I thought I heard voices outside. The clock on the nightstand read 4:02 a.m. I pushed the covers aside and lifted one of the slats in the window blinds. Martin's old green truck was parked by the barn.

"What's going on?" Max came up next to me.

"Isn't it kind of early for Martin to be working?" I asked.

"Ah—I don't think he's working, Jess."

Martin glanced around like he wanted to make sure no one was watching. He then bent down and slid his arms under a man's shoulders and dragged him toward the house.

"He's killed Fred," I gasped. I suddenly knew why Martin had looked so familiar.

"That's not Martin. I mean Martin isn't his real name. That's John Porter—the millionaire my dad is designing a house for." I swallowed hard. John Porter must have been the developer who wanted Amelia's property so badly. And he seemed willing to do anything to get it. He had gone back to the truck and was pulling two gas cans out of the back of his pickup and heading toward the house.

Max jabbed her feet into her tennis shoes. "Jess, we'd better get out of here. You wake up Mrs. T and call the fire department and the sheriff."

"What are you going to do?"

"Head him off at the pass."

"No. You're no match for him."

"If he douses the house with gas, all he has to do is light a match and this place is history." She pulled on a jacket as she left the room. "There's no way the fire department can get here in time."

My heart had slammed into overdrive and I could hardly breathe, let alone talk. I raced into Amelia's room and picked up the phone to call 911. At the same time I shook her awake. Somehow I managed to tell her and the dispatch operator what was going on.

Amelia and I left the house by the front door, which faced the lake. "What about Max?" Amelia started to go back.

"She's outside."

"Jess! Mrs. T!" Max yelled for us from the other side of the house. We ran around to the back porch. I had expected to see flames licking the house by now, but that wasn't happening. Instead, John Porter, alias Martin, was sprawled facedown in the dirt. Molly stood over him barking. Max had Amelia's rifle from the hall closet trained on John's back.

Seeing that Max was okay, Amelia glanced toward the porch where I'd already gone to check on Fred. "Is he . . . ?"

I felt for a pulse and let myself breathe again. "He's alive."

"Thank God." Amelia clasped Max's shoulder and took the gun. "I don't know how you did it, Max, but I'd say you just saved our house and our lives."

Max shrugged. "He wasn't expecting me. Besides, I couldn't have done it without Molly. When I opened the door she charged out and tackled him. It's like she knew what he was doing."

"She probably sensed we were in danger."

"Amelia." John/Martin started to get up. "I can explain. I caught Fred . . ."

"Save your breath." Amelia shoved her slippered foot into his back. "The girls saw everything."

"So you got an offer you couldn't refuse," the sheriff said to Fred once they'd arrested the crooked developer.

We were all sitting in the kitchen while the sheriff questioned us. He'd talked to Amelia, Max, and me first and was trying to figure out where Fred fit into it.

"That's about right." Fred gently touched the gauze bandage wrapped around his head. "Charlie knew he couldn't convince my mother to sell, so he came to me. John Porter had offered three times what the land was worth. At first, I didn't know why he was willing to pay so much, but I later realized he'd known about the mine all along. Carlos must have found out, and Porter killed him."

"So he took on Martin's identity and got the job as Carlos's replacement." Sheriff Clark straddled the chair and took a sip of the coffee Amelia had made.

Fred nodded. "I didn't know he'd killed Carlos until you found the body. That's when I knew I had to come forward. That's why I came here tonight. I had to stop him from destroying the house. I was supposed to rescue you." There were tears in Fred's eyes when he looked up. "I told him the deal was off and to walk away or I would turn him in. A lot of good that did me. He knocked me out and was going to kill all of us in the fire. Martin would then disappear and—well, Sis would have inherited, and she'd have sold the farm in a heartbeat."

Amelia shook her head. "It's too bad Mr. Porter didn't get all of the information," Amelia said. "The mine is worthless."

"No, Mother, it isn't. Porter told me tonight that he had a geological study done. Grandad stopped mining a few feet too soon. There's enough gold in the mine to pay off the farm and mortgages and keep our family in the black for years to come."

I looked over at Max. Her mouth was still hanging open with shock. "Wow, that's great, Mrs. T. You can hire a bunch of people to help out on the farm and to make all your lavender products. You don't have to work at all." Her smile didn't reach her eyes.

"Um—Max." The sheriff looked our way. "I apologize for jumping to conclusions about you, Max. You're a good kid."

"No problem. If you ever need our help solving crimes, don't hesitate to call."

He chuckled. "Never happen." To Fred he said, "You're free to go, but I'll need you to come by the office to give us an official statement."

When the sheriff and Fred had gone home, Amelia said, "I don't know about you girls, but I'm starving. Max, would you like to gather eggs?"

"Sure." Max pushed away from the table. "You want to come with, Jess?"

I did. She didn't talk much while she plucked half a dozen eggs from the nests. On the way back inside, she asked, "Do you think your parents would still let me stay with you guys?"

"Of course!" My happiness shriveled up like a raisin when I saw her expression. "If that's what you want."

"I'm not sure I have a choice. Mrs. T isn't going to want me around now that she's rich. You heard what Freddy said. She sure won't want anyone like me hanging around."

"I don't believe that." I didn't know what else to say. I wanted Max to come back to us, but I also wanted her to be happy.

"You're awfully quiet," Amelia said to Max as she dished up our plates.

"I guess I'm just tired."

"Not too tired to go into town with me, I hope. I need to take some more gift items for the tea shop, and I was hoping you and Jessie could give me a hand. And Jessie, you'll need to bring your things. I promised your mother I'd take you home."

Max frowned. "Why are you doing that? Fred said you were rich and that you don't need to make any more stuff for the shop."

Amelia laughed. "Oh, Max. Fred may be my son, but he doesn't know me at all. I love my lavender fields and creating all the things I can make with the lavender. Working the farm is what keeps me feeling young. Besides, I'm not the kind of person who counts their chickens before they hatch."

"Well, I was thinking about going back to the Millers'. I figure you don't need me anymore."

"Max." Amelia hesitated. "If that's what you really want . . ."

I looked from one to the other and rolled my eyes. I could see where this was going. Amelia and Max would be miserable without each other. "Max thinks you don't want her anymore."

"Jess." Max glowered at me.

Amelia set her napkin down. "Do you still believe I only wanted you for what you could give me in return? Or for the money the state provides?"

Max stared at her plate and pushed her eggs from one side to the other. Apparently she did. I guessed she still had a hard time believing someone could want her just because she's Max.

Amelia sighed. "I'll tell you what, Max. Stay here for three months, and if you still want to live with Jessie and her family after that, I won't try to stop you. In the meantime, any money that comes in from the state will go into a college fund for you. I won't spend a dime of it. You don't have to help me with anything. I enjoyed having you and Jessie work with me, but I did it all before you came and I can do it again."

Max frowned. "So you still want me?"

"Of course."

"Okay, it's a deal." The gap between Max's teeth showed as she broke into a contagious grin. "But only if I can help out around here."

"I'm glad that's settled," I said. "Let's hurry and eat. We have to tell Cooper what happened and let him know you're safe. And

Ivy's party is tonight and we have to get ready."

"Tonight?" Max seemed surprised. "I forgot all about it."

"Are you going?" I asked.

Her eyes lit up. "Sure, but I'd better get busy."

"Why? Busy doing what?"

"Oh, nothing." Her devious expression told me otherwise.

"What are you planning to do?" I was more than a little concerned knowing how Max felt about the other girls who would be there.

She looked me square in the eyes and said, "Don't worry, Jess. I just thought I'd make some lavender cookies."

ACKNOWLEDGMENTS

Thanks to all the children who, over the years, gave me insight into what it means to have a serious and life-threatening illness. Their courage is mirrored in characters like Jessie, Max, and Cooper.

ABOUT THE AUTHOR

Internationally known author and speaker **Patricia H. Rushford** has book sales totaling over a million copies. She has written numerous articles and authored over forty books, including *What Kids Need Most in a Mom, Have You Hugged Your Teenager Today?,* and *It Shouldn't Hurt to be a Kid.* She also writes a number of mystery series: *The Jennie McGrady Mysteries* for kids and the *Helen Bradley Mysteries* for adults. Her latest releases include: *The McAllister Files, She Who Watches, The Angel Delaney Mysteries* with *As Good as Dead* and a romantic suspense, *Sins of the Mother.* Her newest series for children is *The Max & Me Mysteries.*

One of her mysteries, *Silent Witness,* was nominated for an Edgar by Mystery Writers of America and won the Silver Angel for excellence in media. *Betrayed* was selected as best mystery for young adults *The Oregonian* (1997) and won the Phantom Friends Award. *Morningsong,* a romantic suspense, won the Golden Quill for Inspirational Romance award.

Patricia is a registered nurse and holds a Master's Degree in Counseling. In addition, she conducts writers workshops for adults and children and is codirector of *Writer's Weekend at the Beach*. She is the current director of the Oregon Christian Writers Summer Conference. Pat has appeared on numerous radio and television talk shows across the U.S. and Canada. She lives in the Portland, Oregon, area with her husband.

www.patriciarushford.com
Author/Speaker
What Kids Need Most in a Mom
The Jennie Mcgrady Mysteries
The McAllister Files
The Angel Delaney Mysteries
The Helen Bradley Mysteries
The Max & Me Mysteries (New!)

ISBN 10: 0-8024-6254-5
ISBN 13: 978-0-8024-6254-1

ISBN 10: 0-8024-6253-7
ISBN 13: 978-0-8024-6253-4

ISBN 10: 0-8024-6255-3
ISBN 13: 978-0-8024-6255-8

THE MAX & ME MYSTERIES SERIES

From award-winning mystery writer Patricia Rushford comes a new youth mystery series set in Washington state.

The Trouble with Max

Max Hunter and Jessie Miller, two sixth-grade girls living near the Cascade mountains, make an unlikely pair: Jessie has leukemia and is bald. Max dresses like a punk and acts tough in school. But their friendship holds life together when everything else falls apart. Then one day Jessie discovers Max's best-kept secret. Jessie wants to help her, but doing so means risking their friendship.

Danger at Lakeside Farm

Jessie is thin and frail, Max is brave and adventurous, but together they're a great team. Following their first adventure in book one, Max has moved in with an elderly neighbor, Amelia, at Lakeside Farm. Soon strange things start happening at the farm, and Max and Jess wonder if someone wants Amelia out.

Secrets of Ghost Island

Max and Jess discover a family of orphans living on nearby Ghost Island, trying to avoid deportation. The girls decide to help them, when suddenly the town is hit by a rash of burglaries.

by Patricia Rushford

Find them now at your favorite local or online bookstore.

www.MoodyPublishers.com

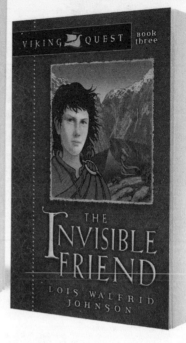

Raiders from the Sea
0-8024-3112-7
978-0-8024-3112-7

Mystery of the Silver Coins
0-8024-3113-5
978-0-8024-3113-4

The Invisible Friend
0-8024-3114-3
978-0-8024-3114-1

Heart of Courage
0-8024-3115-1
978-0-8024-3115-8

The Raider's Promise
0-8024-3116-X
978-0-8024-3116-5

THE VIKING QUEST SERIES

Bree and her brother Devin are kidnapped from 10th century Ireland by Viking raiders. What follows is their dangerous quest to return home as their faith and courage are continually challenged.

by Lois Walfrid Johnson

Find these books now at your favorite local or online bookstore.

www.MoodyPublishers.com

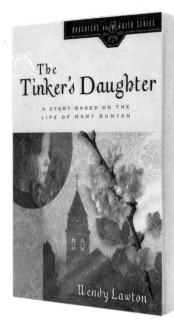
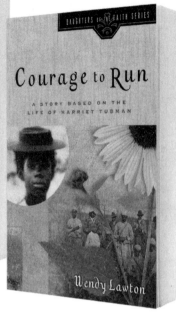

Flight of the Eagles #1
0-8024-3681-1
978-08024-3681-8

The Gates of Neptune #2
0-8024-3682-X
978-08024-3682-5

The Sword of Camelot #3
0-8024-3683-8
978-08024-3683-2

The Caves That Time Forgot #4
0-8024-3684-6
978-08024-3684-9

Winged Raiders of the Desert #5
0-8024-3685-4
978-08024-3685-6

Empress of the Underworld #6
0-8024-3686-2
978-08024-3686-3

Voyage of the Dolphin #7
0-8024-3687-0
978-08024-3687-0

Attack of the Amazons #8
0-8024-3691-9
978-08024-3691-7

Escape with the Dream Maker #9
0-8024-3692-7
978-08024-3692-4

The Final Kingdom #10
0-8024-3693-5
978-08024-3693-1

THE SEVEN SLEEPERS SERIES

Join the adventure with Josh and friends as they are sent by their spiritual leader, Goel, on dangerous and challenging voyages to conquer the forces of darkness in the new world.

by Gilbert Morris

Find these books now at your favorite local or online bookstore.

www.MoodyPublishers.com

The Spell of the Crystal Chair #1
0-8024-3667-6
978-08024-3667-2

The Savage Game of Lord Zarak #2
0-8024-3668-4
978-08024-3668-9

The Strange Creatures of Dr. Korbo #3
0-8024-3669-2
978-08024-3669-6

The City of the Cyborgs #4
0-8024-3670-6
978-08024-3670-2

The Temptations of Pleasure Island #5
0-8024-3671-4
978-08024-3671-9

The Victims of Nimbo #6
0-8024-3672-2
978-08024-3672-6

The Terrible Beast of Zor #7
0-8024-3673-0
978-08024-3673-3

THE LOST CHRONICLES SERIES

Here are more exciting adventures from the Seven Sleepers. As they attempt to faithfully follow Goel, these young people encounter danger, intrigue, and mystery.

by Gilbert Morris

Find these books now at your favorite local or online bookstore.

www.MoodyPublishers.com